THE DOG SOX

THE DOG SOX

a novel by Russell Hill

Caravel Books
an imprint of Pleasure Boat Studio:
A Literary Press
New York

The Dog Sox
by Russell Hill

ISBN 978-1-929355-74-7
Library of Congress Control Number: 2010940151

Cover art by Richard Stine

Caravel Books is a crime and mystery imprint of
Pleasure Boat Studio

Caravel Books and Pleasure Boat Studio books are available through the following:
SPD (Small Press Distribution) Tel. 800-869-7553, Fax 510-524-0852
Partners/West Tel. 425-227-8486, Fax 425-204-2448
Baker & Taylor 800-775-1100, Fax 800-775-7480
Ingram Tel 615-793-5000, Fax 615-287-5429
Amazon.com and **bn.com**

and through
PLEASURE BOAT STUDIO: A LITERARY PRESS
www.pleasureboatstudio.com
201 West 89th Street
New York, NY 10024

Contact Jack Estes
Fax; 888-810-5308
Email: pleasboat@nyc.rr.com

The Dog Sox

In *The Art of Drowning*, Billy Collins (the poet, not the baseball pitcher) wrote,

> . . . if something does flash before your eyes
> as you go under, it will probably be a fish,
> a quick blur of curved silver darting away,
> having nothing to do with your life or your death.

The Knights Landing Dog Sox roster

Darryl Anger, *catcher*

Billy Collins, *pitcher*

Otis Bickford (English teacher, Las Plumas High School), *pitcher*

Barney McChesney (plumber), *pitcher*

Manny Garcia (policeman), *back-up catcher, relief pitcher*

Johnny Hardcase (shop teacher, Maxwell High School), *first base*

Earl Harrington (sophomore, College of the Redwoods) *second base*

Pumpsey Brown, *shortstop*

Dennis Huajardo (farm laborer), *third base*

Paul Credenza, (sheetrocker) *left field*

Joe Johnson (farm equipment mechanic), *center field*

Pete Lubinski (backhoe operator), *right field*

Dutch Goltz, *coach, manager*

Ray Adams, *general manager*

Ava Belle, *owner*

Jack, *the dog*

Chapter 1

They were called The Dog Sox. Not the White Sox or the Black Sox or the Red Sox, but the Dog Sox. Because the guy who bought the team liked dogs and he had dogs embroidered on his shorts and a dog following him around and he had a pair of socks given to him by a beautiful woman who, in the heat of the moment, thought they would look good on his naked feet that had tiny dogs on them. On the socks, not his feet. So he gave the woman the team. She liked baseball and she liked sitting in the owner's box, which wasn't actually a box. It was a folding chair behind home plate, behind the netting that kept foul balls from ricocheting off the crowd. Which wasn't much of a crowd. Still, on a soft summer night in Knight's Landing, under the dim glow of the lights from the three outfield poles, it had the feel of real baseball, and she drove two hours from San Francisco to sit in that folding chair and have a Trout Slayer beer.

When Ray Adams bought the Knights Landing Dredgers he renamed them the Dog Sox. There was a black lab on the cap of each player and he hired a kid from Yuba City High School to climb into a costume and prance around the field. It was a black dog costume and if you squinted your eyes you could imagine that it was a big dog and not a kid in a dog suit. The head was pretty realistic and the big moment was when the dog went over to the backstop net and pawed his way around it to the folding chair and laid down next to the woman who owned the team so she could pat him on his head. And then he would whip off the dog's head and sit up and she would lean forward and kiss him on the forehead and the crowd, all eighty-five of them, would erupt in a cheer.

Of course, what she didn't realize was that the kid cherished that moment more than the crowd did, because when she bent forward to kiss him on the forehead he got to look down her blouse at her tits, and sometimes she had on this black bra that didn't really cover them all that well, and then he put the dog head back on and went wild. The crowd, such as it was, cheered again and the woman clapped her hands, but what nobody else knew was that the kid was trying not to come inside the dog suit.

Chapter 2

The guy who bought the team didn't sit in the owner's box. He worked the hot dog booth and sold beer and chased baseballs that got hit out of the park because the budget didn't allow for unlimited balls. Grade school kids who found a ball and brought it back got a free Coke. He suspected that the kid in the dog suit was trying to work off a hard-on after the ceremonial kiss, but he didn't mention it to the woman. She had spiky auburn hair with a hint of red in it and green eyes and sometimes she wore a silk blouse to the games and sometimes it was a cashmere vee-neck sweater and always she wore Levis and often she kicked off her shoes and went barefoot, walking back after the game to the dirt parking lot next to the river carrying her shoes in one hand and the beer bottle in the other.

Some nights they didn't drive back to San Francisco, staying at an old motel in Knight's Landing in unit #6, a room that had a single table, a bed next to the wall with a window facing the river, and a narrow kitchen where, in the morning, he made coffee and omelets and watched her stir in her sleep, her arms outstretched, her shoulders moving gently to the rhythm of her breathing.

When she woke she lay for a while, watching him as he made the coffee, and when he brought her a cup she sat up, naked, cradling the white mug with both hands and he wanted to leap into the bed, spread her legs, bury his face between her thighs, but he stood at the edge of the bed and she sipped at the coffee and said, "Last night. Billy Collins."

"The pitcher."

"We got anybody else on the team named Billy Collins?"

"I'll give you a pass on that because you just woke up."

"You ever see anybody pitch like that?"

"Like what?"

"A sidearm that comes off the mound and damn near touches the ground? It comes up off his feet and it looks like some kind of softball pitch but it's 90 miles an hour and nobody could hit him. I mean fucking nobody." She put the coffee cup on the table next to her.

"You'd like to fuck me again, wouldn't you?" she said. "You ever get enough?"

"No."

"I thought not. " She put her legs over the side of the bed and stood up.

"I'm going to take a shower and when I come out I want you to tell me everything you know about Billy Collins." She went into the little bathroom that was scabbed onto the side of the unit and he heard the shower go on and he thought about taking his clothes off and joining her in the shower but he thought better of it. Don't push it, some little voice in his lizard brain was saying. Make her that omelet and make her another cup of coffee and try to remember where Billy Collins comes from.

When he heard the shower stop he cracked the eggs and dropped them into a bowl, whipping them with a fork. She appeared in the doorway of the kitchen wearing a white shirt of his, unbuttoned. That was all she was wearing and he thought, Jesus, if I could afford the New York Yankees, I would buy them for her.

"Billy Collins," she said. "Where did Dutch find him?"

He dropped the eggs into the pan, tipping it so that they covered the surface.

"He pitched high school ball up on the North Coast. Fortuna, I think. Then he did a season for College of the Redwoods. Dutch saw him one night pitching for the Humboldt Crabs, a semi-pro team in Arcata. He told me it was like watching a freak show."

"And it's okay to pitch like that? There's no rule that you can't throw that way?"

"You can throw the ball any way you want as long as you put one foot on the rubber." He pulled the edge of the egg into the center of the pan with the fork, tipping the pan again so that the uncooked egg slid onto the hot surface. He dropped some cheese into the pan, added, and a few pieces of Canadian bacon, folding the egg over with the fork. Turning the pan, he slid the omelet onto a warm plate.

"Your breakfast, O princess of the fastball."

She took the plate into the room with the bed, setting it on the table.

"When I finish," she said, sipping the hot coffee he had set next to her plate, "you get to pitch again. We'll see what kind of stuff you've got." She took his hand, raising it to cup her breast. "Maybe you ought to warm up," she said. "I wouldn't want you to pull a muscle or anything."

Chapter 3

Dutch Goltz wasn't Dutch. He was a Jewish boy who had been called that when he was a kid because he was in and out of trouble all the time, and his father's brother used an expression, "That kid is always in dutch," and it stuck. By the time he was eighteen he was a left-handed power hitter and he got drafted by the Oakland A's and played several seasons for the Stockton Ports. He got called up once, late in the season, but he couldn't hit a big league curve ball. He took a job coaching a semi-pro team in San Jose and Dutch discovered that he could handle young ballplayers, bring them along, make a team out of cast-offs, and he hung around the fringes of baseball for the next thirty-five years, working off-season as a carpenter or a truck driver and finding a team to coach during the summer months. Once it was a single-A club in the Texas panhandle and, now that he had passed seventy, it was the Knight's Landing Dog Sox. He didn't hide his distaste for the team name, but he had managed to assemble a roster of players that could go nine innings without embarrassing him or the fans.

Of the nine starters, three were paid a salary: $2500 a month to three kids who were hoping that a scout would come to a game and they would leave a league that played sheetrockers and high school dropouts. Pumpsey Brown, the shortstop, had played college ball for USC. He was the only black player on the team, and he said he was the reincarnation of Ricky Henderson. Dutch had to sit on him to keep him from trying to steal every time he got on base. Darryl Anger, the catcher, played for the Sonoma Crushers for two seasons before the team folded, and he was steady, a good hitter, a bulk of a target behind the plate, with a quiet demeanor that some would have called withdrawn, but Dutch knew that Darryl kept a book on every batter they faced and the wheels were turning inside his square head all the time. Four games into the season, Dutch took Billy Collins out of the rainy North Coast where he worked for Marconi's Fish Products during the day and played for Marconi's Humboldt Crabs at night. Dutch had never seen a motion like Billy's and at first he thought it was just a freak thing, but the more he watched, the more he liked what he saw. For three or four innings the kid was unhittable. Then he turned wild but Dutch figured that he could tame the kid, get seven innings out of him, and he offered him a contract. When Dutch told Billy he would never again smell like fish guts and he would actually get paid to play ball, he was packed and on the road. Billy and Darryl and Pumpsey lived in a rented house in Woodland, twenty miles from Knight's Landing, ate off the dollar menu at McDonalds, and were the heart of Dutch's team.

The others were part-time ballplayers who got fifty bucks a game. Some of them harbored illusions that a scout would see them and they would suddenly be in Triple-A ball, while others just wanted to play baseball, knew they were also-rans, but liked the idea that they could put on a uniform and stand under the lights on a Friday or a Saturday night and hear the crack of the bat.

Chapter 4

"The thing is," Dutch said, "the ball comes at you from an angle you just don't like. Look at it this way. Ninety-five percent of all pitchers, lefties or right, makes no difference, release the ball shoulder-high. So it comes down at the plate. The other five percent bring their motion off to the side a bit and release chest high. The ball comes in at you pretty much on the level. But this freaking kid brings that ball up off the ground and when he releases it, it's not much more than ankle-high and it rises toward the plate and nobody, and I mean nobody, has spent a career hitting pitches that come up like that. There's maybe a dozen sidearmers in the majors because it puts a helluva strain on your shoulder and sidearmers come apart at the seams. Very few owners want to take a chance on a pitcher who's going to throw his arm out of the socket. And they never have anything on the off-speed pitches. Which means most sidearmers have maybe one or two pitches, but this kid has a curve ball, and it doesn't just break right or left, it breaks right and up or left and up. You've spent years watching a curve drop away or down and now the frigging ball comes up and you swing and you thought it was in the sweet spot and no, it's inside on the letters. And his change-up looks like smoke, but all of a sudden it just isn't there yet. Not because it's such a frigging good change-up, but because it's rising like some space ship taking off. I swear, with a motion like that, he should tear his shoulder right out of the socket. You watch him, and it's this roundhouse that swoops down and then it's David's slingshot. He doesn't look like any sidearmer or submariner I ever saw, and I been watching pitchers for forty years. He gets tired after maybe four innings, so I'm working on his arm strength, but right now, I got a pitcher who goes four innings and faces twelve batters, and all they do is swing at empty air."

Chapter 5

Ray bought the Dog Sox for Ava as a birthday present. It was a rainy January day when he met her at the Stockton Garage in San Francisco. She came out of the elevator wearing a black sweater, black silk scarf, black slacks, and black cowboy boots. She wore silver earrings and her hair was tucked under a black baseball cap. A shiny black raincoat was thrown over her shoulders.

"Mysterious woman in black," Ray said.

"You got that right," she said. "So where are we going?"

"Tiffany's."

"Breakfast at Tiffany's?" Her face lit up. "I like the sound of that."

At eleven o'clock there was no one else in Tiffany's except the clerks and a heavy-set man at the doorway who, Ray suspected, was armed. He smiled at them and a man in a dark suit and an impeccably knotted red tie greeted them.

"We'd like to look at necklaces," Ray said.

Ava took the scarf from around her neck and pointed to one in the case. "I like emeralds," she said. The clerk unlocked the case, brought out the necklace, and stepped behind Ava so he could drape it around her neck and fix the clasp. When he stepped back she looked into the mirror. "Too many diamonds," she said. "It's not subtle enough."

Another necklace materialized. Ray casually looked at the price tag on the first necklace as the clerk laid it on a tray behind the counter. It was more than a hundred grand.

They continued for another half hour until Ava turned to Ray and said, "What I need is a dress to go with this one." She reached up and unclasped it and handed it back to the clerk. "We'll go up the street to Saks," she said. She smiled at the clerk and Ray suppressed a grin. Her smile was that of a rich woman who knows she can have anything she wants and the man next to her is good for it. Suddenly, Ray felt rich.

As they went out the door, the heavy-set guard nodded amiably. Outside, Ava turned to him.

"Nothing? Not even a charm bracelet? What the fuck was that all about?"

"It was about being rich enough to buy you a necklace that costs a fortune."

"You don't have a fucking fortune, Ray. I thought I was going to get a birthday present!"

"You are," he said. "That was the teaser." He reached out and turned her toward Stockton Street. "First we have a glass of champagne."

They turned at the corner, went up the hill to Campton Place and went past the doorman, through the gold and glass doors into the quietly rich lobby. A few steps down into the small bar and they were alone.

The champagne wasn't cheap. Two glasses of Veuve Cliquot set Ray back thirty dollars. He raised his flute, touched hers, and laid the envelope on the bar.

"What's this?" she said.

"Open it and see."

She unclasped the brown manila envelope and took out the papers. She examined them and then turned to him. "This says I own a baseball team," she said. "When did that happen?"

"Last week. I bought you the Knight's Landing Dredgers. Only now they're named the Dog Sox."

She burst into laughter.

"Are you out of your mind?"

"You love baseball. I love dogs. You are the owner of a baseball team. Named the Dog Sox. The mascot is a black lab."

"Jesus, Ray, what did this set you back?"

"Not that much."

"No, that won't do. You don't have a lot of money, Ray. You're a general contractor and you do things like remodel a kitchen, which you did for me, so I want to know what you did."

"Less than your kitchen."

"That's no answer."

"I bought the name and the right to play ball in a rickety stadium in a little town in the Central Valley and the first month's contracts on three ball players, the manager's salary and enough hot dogs and Cokes for five games. After that we depend on tickets and hot dogs and luck. You're the owner. You get to sit in the owner's box and act like a rich woman. You carry yourself like one. You looked so fucking rich in Tiffany's I thought that salesman was going to have an orgasm. I bought you a baseball club for your birthday, Ava."

She fingered the paper, raised her champagne to her lips and took a sip.

"You are full of surprises, Ray Adams. You take me to Tiffany's, let me try on diamonds and emeralds, and then you give me a baseball team. So what do we do now?"

"We finish this." He raised his glass to touch hers again. "And then we go upstairs in this fancy hotel and the owner of the Knight's Landing Dog Sox and the general manager who also is the hot dog cooker, will have their first strategy meeting."

"Is there an agenda?" she asked.

"Mostly it involves you wearing a lot less than what you have on now."

"Pretty sure of yourself, aren't you?"

"Reasonably sure. It's not every day I get to bed the owner of a baseball team. I want to make the most of it."

"So what will it cost you for a late-morning fuck with this baseball owner?"

"If you count the ball club and the champagne and the room, maybe a couple of thousand an hour."

"You think I'm worth that much?"

"Worth every penny," he said.

Chapter 6

They traveled to Oroville to play the Steelhead. The ballpark was better than the Knight's Landing park. There were not only light poles in the outfield, but two along each baseline, and there were nearly 500 people in the stands. Word had gotten out that there was a freak pitcher for the Dog Sox that nobody could hit. The home team got to keep seventy-five percent of the gate and all of the concession stand take, but five hundred tickets at four bucks apiece meant that the Sox went home with enough to cover the payroll for the night.

Pumpsey led off the first inning with a walk, stole second even though there was no sign, and the pitcher was rattled enough to walk the second batter, a right fielder named Pete Lubinski who was, during the day, a back-hoe operator for a construction company. Darryl Anger crushed the next pitch over the left field fence into a rice field and Billy Collins had a three-run lead in the bottom of the first. Watching Billy pitch was like watching somebody eat fireworks. He stood there on the mound and looked intently at Darryl and when he got the sign he nodded and then he rose, his skinny body like some kind of an egret or a heron, up on his toes, his long neck stretched, chin up, looking down his beak at the batter, and then his right arm went out above his head and it came down in a roundhouse curve behind his back, his body rolling into the motion, left foot as high as the top of his head, and the arm came down at the same time as the leg and his hand swept the ground, only inches from the dirt, and he released the ball, striding forward, following through with so much power that the ball seemed to skip, and then there was the pop! as it hit Darryl's mitt and the batter adjusted himself, pretending that he hadn't liked that pitch, but the fact was he had no idea where or when it had crossed the plate. Three batters. If they swung at a pitch it was a half-hearted swing and, with the third out, Billy punched his fist into his mitt, an exclamation point as he went back to the dugout, and Dutch thought, *Oy vey*! I've got a Golem here. Some kind of thing made by the rabbi out of dust in the attic of the synagogue, and if I can learn the secret words I've got the magic that I have been looking for all my life.

Chapter 7

Ray stopped in Yuba City and bought fireworks from a roadside stand the week before the 4th of July. He bought two hundred dollars worth of rockets and brought them back to Knight's Landing. He asked Maria Lopez at the Taqueria if she knew a couple of guys who would light them for him during the seventh inning stretch of the Friday night game. He would pay them twenty bucks apiece and Maria said her husband and his brother would do it. So Friday night on the 4th of July weekend, Jose and Escobar Lopez showed up and carried the boxes of fireworks out beyond the left field fence to the parking lot next to the rice silos.

"Remember," Ray told them, "don't start until you hear the music."

The Dog Sox were ahead by two runs in the top of the seventh, and Barney McChesney, the plumber from Chico who had played a season of single-A ball in the Arizona League right out of high school, had taken over after Billy began to fall apart in the fifth inning. Barney put them down in order in the top of the seventh, and Ray put the disc in the player at the back of the snack shop and turned the loudspeakers all the way up.

The speakers crackled and then the 1812 Overture blasted out, fuzzy and distorted, and Ray looked out toward the rice silos. There was nothing and he thought that Jose and Escobar had flaked on him when suddenly the sky lit up. Somehow they had fused all of the rockets together and they went up in a constant stream, filling the night sky with gun shots and fiery bursts and, instead of a fireworks display that should have lasted fifteen minutes, the whole show was over in less than a minute, a blitzkrieg of explosion and sparks trailing down. And then the rocket that had lodged in the eucalyptus trees at the edge of the river exploded and in short order the tree exploded in a column of fire, and then the next tree, and the one after that.

Holy shit! Ray thought, and the crowd cheered. He heard the volunteer fire department siren go off and then came the siren of the town's single pumper truck, mixed with Tchaikovsky's cannons and trumpets. The wall of trees was a mass of red and orange and black smoke towering above the river, and then they flared and died and he could see the stream of water from the pumper playing on the trees but it was no more than an exercise for the volunteers. The stand of trees turned black and the crowd settled back for the finish of the game.

"Fucking-A, Mr. Adams, that was the best fireworks I ever saw." It was the mascot. He'd taken off his dog suit, collected his ten dollars, and was drinking his free Coke.

Ray left the snack shop and found Ava sipping her beer in her folding chair.

"You are out of your mind," she said.

"I planned it that way."

"Bullshit!"

"No need to get vulgar. That was for you."

"I suppose you want to spend the night here."

"It crossed my mind."

"Will there be any more fireworks?"
"You never know," he said.

* * * * * *

When she came, there was an explosion in her body, and she cried out and then she was still, until she shuddered, as if she were trying to shake off something. It was the kind of involuntary movement his grandmother would have explained with "someone walked over your grave."

And she was asleep, one arm stretched above her head, her face resting on her arm, hair a wild spikiness, the other arm limp across her thigh. Her breath slowed and he watched the almost imperceptible rise and fall of her back. He came closer to her until their bodies touched, reached across to rest his hand on her breast, felt her heart beating, and waited.

Chapter 8

Ray's dog traveled everywhere with him. It was a nondescript dog that he got at the pound, saving it from being put down, which Ray felt gave him some points somewhere on somebody's checklist. It was part Australian sheepdog and part something else because it had short brown-and-white hair and a long nose. Maybe some heeler in it, the kid at the pound had said. Ray had different names for him. Sometimes he called him Roundup because he had a penchant for herding, going after small groups of kids on a playground or working a flock of seagulls on the beach. Other times Ray called him Partner because he was close enough to fit that name. He rode in the cab of Ray's truck to jobs, sitting in the passenger's seat, moving over to the driver's seat when Ray got out, sitting there as if he were about to drive off but was wondering where he would go. But the name that Ray used most of the time was Jack. Ray remembered a book from his childhood by Albert Payson Terhune titled *Real Tales of Real Dogs*, filled with stories of dogs that traveled across the world to find their lost master or faced a lion to save a woman in the African veldt or plunged into a raging river to save a child. One of the dogs in that book was named Jack. Unlike the other heroic dogs, Jack had been a rather unassuming dog who ran through a hail of bullets to take a message to headquarters. Ray wasn't sure that his Jack would do that. But he liked the idea.

So when Ray went to a ball game in Knight's Landing with Ava, Jack came too. He didn't like sitting in the back seat of Ava's Beemer. He lay on the seat, a mournful expression on his face. He liked Ray's truck because he could see what was coming up next and, if the weather was warm, Ray left the window open, and Jack stuck his head out into the slipstream, his eyes closed because of the rice bugs that swarmed in the Valley.

At the ballpark, Jack sat underneath the propane cooker, and every once in a while Ray said, "This isn't good for you. Don't tell anyone," and he took a small chunk of hot dog and dropped it at his feet.

"Does it bother you that this is called a hot dog?" he asked.

Jack didn't say anything, just neatly mouthed the chunk of meat and swallowed.

When they went to the motel, Jack curled up in the bathroom. Ray maintained that Jack was a dog with a sense of decorum. "He doesn't want to be a pain in the neck," Ray said. "He knows that if he's in the same room when you and I are fucking, it would put a damper on things. So he goes in there because he's got a sensitive nature."

"It's warmer in there," Ava said. She was sitting naked on top of Ray, straddling him, reaching back to cup her hands at the back of her head. "We took a shower and the steam warmed things up and he likes it. Don't tell me he's sensitive to the fact that you want to fuck my lights out."

"If you want to be crude about it," Ray said, "be my guest. My dog would never say that. He wouldn't even think it."

"If there were six of me in here," Ava said, "your dog would be nipping at my heels, trying to get all six of me in the corner of the room."

"If there were six of you," Ray said, "I would be in deep trouble. I would need his help."

Chapter 9

The rest of the team consisted of guys who did other things for a living. Pete Lubinski ran a backhoe. Manny Garcia was a cop in Oroville. He was a big man with a big gut who was a backup catcher and could pitch an inning or two because he had an arm that threw rifle shots. He had only one pitch, a fastball that had the same velocity as the legendary Bob Feller, and control that was on the shaky side, which was why opposing batters didn't crowd the plate. Paul Credenza was the left fielder. Paul had been a high-school all star, but now he had six kids and a wife who cut him loose on Friday and Saturday nights only because he brought in a hundred bucks in cash. "That's what happens when you swing your dick instead of your bat," Paul said.

Third base was Dennis Huajardo, who was a farm laborer and had played ball in Puerto Rico and held out the hope that a scout would see him and he would be the next Orlando Cepeda. He had quick hands, could turn a double play so fast it was a blur, but he wanted to get hits so badly that he kept going after bad pitches. Dutch figured that if he never swung at all, he would get on base every time on a walk, since opposing pitchers knew his penchant for reaching for outside balls. Dennis swung anyway, and sometimes he connected with one of those pitches and it was enough to surprise the infield.

First base was Johnny Hardcase, who was six-four and scooped up anything that came within three yards of the bag. Johnny was a shop teacher at Maxwell High School just off Interstate 5, a tiny high school of 175 students with a football team and a rodeo team. Kids came to school in pickups with a loaded gun rack in the cab.

By July, the team had a 10-2 record and was in first place in the Central Valley League.

Chapter 10

The Snack Shack was a box beneath the stands with a fold-up hatch that revealed a wooden counter and a dimly lit interior where there was a propane cooker and an ancient disc player that was connected to the outside loudspeakers. The menu consisted of hot dogs and candy bars and Cokes and Trout Slayer beer. Ray had a pot of weiners in hot water that he lifted with a pair of tongs, put on a bun and sold for a buck and a half. At the end of the counter were bottles of ketchup and mustard. Nothing else. He got the idea of offering burritos when he stopped for one at Maria Lopez' taqueria on the highway that ran through town. She was a big woman with a perpetual smile and they worked out a deal. She would sell fat burritos stuffed with pork and beans and cheese and rice for three dollars and the team would get to keep fifty cents. The first night they tried it she sold a hundred and the Dog Sox pocketed fifty dollars. Maria was happy. So was Ray.

The night after the 4th of July fireworks a man showed up at the open hatch.

"What'll you have?" Ray asked.

The man was unshaven and unsteady, a greasy shirt and a

greasier baseball cap. Stringy hair sprouted from the edges of the cap.

"You the guy what owns the team?" he asked.

"No, the owner is a woman. What do you want?"

"Then I want to talk to her."

"You can talk to me. I'm the general manager."

"Fancy title for the hot dog man on a piss-ant ball club," the man said, the edge of his mouth lifting to show stained teeth.

Jack raised his head and began to growl.

"You got a problem, spill it," Ray said. "I got things to do."

Behind and above him there was a cheer. Billy Collins had ended a third inning of no-hit ball.

"That kid that's pitching," the man said, "is my kid. I raised him."

Ray took a closer look. There seemed to be no resemblance between Billy and this unsteady drunk.

"You don't say."

"I fucking do say. And I think you're gonna make a deal with me."

"What kind of a deal?"

"You or your cunt owner are gonna sell him to some big league team and you're gonna get a shitload of money and, as his old man, I'm entitled to a cut."

"One," Ray said, "is that I don't know if you are who you say you are. Two, Billy is over eighteen so you don't have a fucking claim to anything. And three, you come here and threaten me and you'll get your ass kicked all the way back to whatever hole you crawled out of."

"My name is Bucky Collins," the man said. "You threaten me and I'll burn your fucking ballpark to the ground." He half turned and then said, "I think I'll go find the pussy who owns this shithole."   Ray turned to Maria.

"Keep an eye on things, will you?" and he went out the side door after the man. He didn't see him so he went directly to the chair behind home plate where Ava sat. The chair was empty. He waited, looking for the man, trying to spot Ava, and then he saw her leaving the portable toilet behind the left field line.

When she got to Ray she said, "How about another beer?"

"Did a greasy drunk find you?"

"Not unless he was in there watching me pee."

"There's a drunk here who claims to be Billy Collins' father. He's a nasty piece of work and he said he was going to find you."

"What does he want with me?"

"He says we're going to sell Billy to the majors for a pile of money and he wants a cut."

"Are we selling Billy to the majors?"

"Not that I know of. But this jerkoff threatened to burn down the ballpark and he smells like trouble. If he finds you, come and find me."

Ava sat down and picked up the empty beer bottle that was next to the chair. "Bring me a full one of these. If he tries anything, I'll clock him with it."

"I'm serious," Ray said.

"So am I," Ava replied.

Chapter 11

There was no sign of Bucky Collins the rest of the night. He didn't approach Ava and he didn't show up at the Snack Shack. Ray made the rounds during the top of the seventh, but he wasn't in the stands and he wasn't hanging around the graveled parking lot. Apparently he had taken a powder.

When the game was over, the lights had dimmed and then gone out on the outfield poles, and Ray and Ava were counting the take, Dutch showed up.

"Good night?" he asked.

"Every time Billy pitches it's a good night. They come out of the woodwork. We sold five hundred and eleven tickets, Maria sold more than a hundred burritos, beer was good, and we came out with better than twenty-five hundred cash. Take away the cost of beer and hot dogs and we go home with twenty-three hundred dollars. Which pays for you, Dutch, and the three contract players and fifty bucks each for the rest and that leaves enough to pay the motel for me and Ava tonight. You want a beer on the house? One for the road?"

"No," Dutch said. "But I got something you ought to know."

"Which is?"

"Billy Collins has a father. He showed up tonight. He's bad news."

"Greasy drunk?"

"You met him?"

"He came by. Said if we sold Billy to the Bigs he wanted a cut. I told him to fuck off."

"He showed up in the dugout," Dutch said. "You would have thought Billy saw a ghost. The drunk told me who he was and I asked Billy if that was true and Billy just buried his face in his hands, which was why he didn't pitch the fourth inning. He acted like he got a line drive in the gut. I told the guy that only ball players were allowed in the dugout and he had to clear out. He told me to kiss his ass, so I had Manny escort him out. My guess is that Manny didn't follow proper police procedures."

"What did Billy say?"

"Not much. He hasn't seen his old man in more than three years. Apparently he used to beat the shit out of Billy's mother and Billy, too, until Billy got big enough to fight back. "

"Is he going to be all right?"

"I don't know. He just sat there in the dugout the rest of the game. I told Pumpsey and Darryl to keep a close eye on him when they got back to the house."

"You think Billy can still pitch if this asshole shows up again?"

"I have no idea, Ray." He paused. "On second thought, I will have that beer. You two clear out of here. I'll lock things up."

Cicadas buzzed in the trees next to the parking lot and mosquitoes whined. As Ray got into the car, he looked back.

There was no light in the ballpark except for the open hatch of the Snack Shack. He could see the upper half of Dutch standing in the opening, drinking his beer.

Chapter 12

The roadway on the bridge over the Sacramento at the north end of Knight's Landing was a metal grid and the tires hummed as they crossed it. The town was only a quarter of a mile long, and then the highway curved west toward Woodland. It was hot and Ray was hungry and he stopped opposite the Mexican restaurant. Big signs announced BURRITOS, TAMALES. The burritos were big, wrapped in a warm soft tortilla that Maria Lopez made. He was still across the street when it happened.

Just as he reached for the door handle, a passing ranch truck hit a dog. It was a big pickup towing a farm trailer and the dog was into the road before the driver saw it. There was an audible thump as the dog went under the front wheel. It pinwheeled under the truck, only to be struck solidly by the trailer, which kicked it out the back end. The rancher stopped and got out, leaving his truck in the middle of the road, engine still running. The dog lay on the pavement and it struggled to get up, get its front legs under it, but the back half of the body stayed put. The dog looked perplexed and it whined and the man called to it. He wore a baseball cap, a blue chambray work shirt, jeans and dusty work boots, and he must have been in his sixties.

"Come on, boy," he called. The dog looked in his direction and shifted its front legs so that it moved toward his voice, but the rest of the dog was someplace else, disconnected in some way, and then Ray could see the woman with the child on the far side, the child holding onto the woman's leg, face buried in the woman's ample thigh, and the woman wasn't moving. She stood, motionless, a bag of groceries in one arm and he thought, it's her dog. Or at least she knows the dog. It was a bulldog of some kind, maybe thirty or forty pounds, a stocky dog, but now it seemed somehow elongated and the man called out again. Ray thought, he knows better than to go near an injured animal and he's trying to see if things will re-connect and the dog will get up. But the dog whined again and now it put its head on the pavement for a moment, lifting it to look toward the voice of the man. Enough, Ray said to himself. He was no longer hungry. He started the motor, pulled out and went toward the bridge. He did not look back.

The road through the valley was two lanes, rice fields and tomato fields on the sides, sometimes egrets picking their way along the edge of the road in the irrigation ditches. What would the rancher do? There was no doubt in Ray's mind that the man had dogs of his own. He stood there, calling to the dog, hoping it would rise, like Lazarus, be whole again. And he knew it would not.

How quickly it happens. Ray said, and he realized he was speaking out loud, talking to his dog, Jack, who sat in the passenger's seat looking out at the barren fields. One minute you're talking with a friend, sipping a scotch in a dark bar, and the next minute the bolt of lightning comes through your brain and you, too, lie on the pavement, unable to comprehend where you are. Someone is calling to you, hoping that you'll rise and be whole again.

Not you, Jack, he said. You don't drink scotch.

An egret stood in an empty rice field, a solitary white brush stroke. There was smoke in the valley. They were burning off the rice stubble in preparation for the next year's planting. The woman would have to get another dog.

An old pickup truck came at him, half over the line, and Ray blinked his lights, tapped the horn. The truck slid back into its lane and went past, and Ray pulled over where a farm road intersected the highway. He sat there, the engine ticking over, and thought about Bucky Collins. Maybe Bucky Collins would stop in Knight's Landing to get a burrito and he would step into the road just as some rancher came by towing a trailer and, like the dog, he'd disappear under the front wheel of the truck.

Ray pulled the car onto the road, made a U-turn and headed back toward Knight's Landing.

Chapter 13

Dutch started Billy Collins in the Friday night game, but after three pitches he knew something was wrong. The first batter hit a screamer between third and short and the next batter dropped a Texas leaguer in shallow left field. Pumpsey couldn't get back fast enough and Paul couldn't get in. Men on first and third and the next man up leaned into Billy's fastball, which wasn't all that fast, just seemed to hang there in front of the guy and the score was three-zip, no outs. Dutch called time and walked out to the mound where Billy stood, punching the ball into his mitt. Darryl joined them. Behind Dutch, Manny Garcia was warming up along the right field line.

"Your arm okay?" Dutch asked.

"It's fine," Billy said.

Dutch turned to Darryl. "You see anything wrong?"

"He doesn't have his stuff," Darryl said.

"So what's the problem?" Dutch asked Billy.

"I don't know."

"You look pissed off," Dutch said.

"I'm not pissed off."

"You been going to yoga?"

The plate umpire joined them on the mound. "You guys gonna gab all night or do we play ball?" he said.

Dutch turned to him. "We're going to play ball," he said. "And I'm bringing in a new pitcher and this young man and I are going to have a few more words so my new pitcher can get the kinks out of his arm and I would appreciate it if you would take your fat ass back behind home plate."

"Don't get smart with me, Dutch, or I'll give you the toss."

"You do that," Dutch said, "and when you get to your car after the game you'll probably need to start thinking about some new tires. You don't live in Knight's Landing."

"You got one more minute," the umpire said as he turned back toward the plate.

"So, Billy, this got anything to do with your old man?"

"Fuck him," Billy said.

"That's what I thought," Dutch said. He motioned to Manny who trotted toward the mound. Dutch took the ball from Billy's hand, placed it in Manny's mitt, and said to Darryl, "Nothing but fastballs, and keep him inside. I don't want anybody crowding the plate."

He turned to Manny. "And keep them down. I don't want anybody hit in the head."

"You want me to hit somebody?" Manny asked.

"I want you to throw smoke and I want them to stay nervous. They know you. You hit somebody and you'll get a couple of free innings." He put an arm around Billy's waist.

"Some nights just don't work out," he said. "Nothing to worry about."

But Dutch knew that he did have something to worry about. The magic was beginning to come apart at the seams.

Chapter 14

The next night, Billy sat at the far end of the bench, talking to no one, and nobody sat near him. It was as if he had some kind of contagious air about him that would infect another ballplayer and nobody wanted whatever Billy had to rub off on them. Finally Dutch sat next to him.

"You religious, Billy?" he asked. "Go to church?"

Billy said nothing.

"I'm a Jew," Dutch said. "But you probably know that. I've been going to the synagogue since I was a kid. We don't read the Bible. We read from the Torah. It tells us how to act. There's a story there about a man who tells some lies about his rabbi. Then he realizes he's done something bad and he goes to the rabbi and asks the rabbi to forgive him. The rabbi tells him to go get a feather pillow, cut it open and scatter the feathers in the wind. Why do that? the man asks. Because, the rabbi tells him, you would have to gather up every feather before you would undo the damage you did with your lies."

Billy looked sideways at him. "I don't get it," he said.

"Your old man did some bad things to you and your

mother. He would have to cut up a dozen pillows and then find every feather before he could undo what he's done. Only he's not about to do that. And you can't wait for him to do that."

"He used to beat up my mother when he was drunk," Billy said. "He'd get drunk and he'd start to shout and swear and then he'd start throwing things. And then he would start in on her." Billy's voice had dropped to a whisper but he kept his eyes on the field.

"Some men do that. There's no excuse for it. He beat on you?"

"Until I was sixteen. Then I was big enough to hit back and he left me alone. But he didn't leave her alone."

"So what did you do?"

"Not enough."

"You're not responsible, Billy. You can't gather up the feathers for him. Or for her."

Billy was silent. On the field Barney McChesney was in trouble. He had pitched seven innings and at the top of the eighth the Dog Sox were ahead by one run, but he had men on first and second with one out.

"A double play would be nice right about now," Dutch said.

He stood and motioned to the plate umpire. "Time," he called. The umpire stepped back and lifted both hands. McChesney looked toward the dugout.

"You think you could close out for us, Billy?" Dutch asked.

"I don't know."

"Well, we'll find out. Go throw a few warm-ups while I go out and have a chat with Barney."

Dutch stretched his chat as long as he could until Billy was loose enough, then motioned for him to come in.

"Good job, Barney," Dutch said, taking the ball from him

and dropping it in Billy's outstretched mitt.

"Five batters, kid."

Billy shrugged his shoulders, as if to loosen them.

"Don't try to overpower anybody. Use your curve. You know that yoga position they call the downward dog?"

Billy looked at him in disbelief. "You know that one?" he asked.

"I know a lot of useless shit," Dutch said. "You know that position?"

"It's the one where I put my hands on the floor and my butt in the air."

"That's it. Right now, you're the downward dog. You're the Dog Sox ace, and you're going to go down toward that plate and all you're going to think about is the ball and that hole in the center of the plate where the ball passes through. Nothing else. You understand?"

Billy nodded.

Oy vey, Dutch thought. Let him get this first batter out. Let him be David with his slingshot facing the twelve-foot Goliath. Let his anger work for him the way it worked for David.

Behind the plate Ava leaned forward in her chair. Something was happening out there on the mound and she could feel it. She watched as Dutch went back to the dugout. Billy threw his first warmup and it skipped in the dirt before the plate. Darryl trapped it against his chest, stood, and threw the ball back to Billy. He slapped his mitt, crouched and waited. The next pitch didn't hit the dirt, but it didn't pop in his mitt the way Darryl expected. He looked toward the dugout but Dutch wasn't paying any attention.

The third pitch hopped a bit and Darryl felt better. He held up his hand and when the next pitch came in, a fastball that made a satisfying whack! in his mitt, Darryl threw to second.

Mack took the ball at the bag, shoveled it to Pumpsey who tossed it back to Billy.

Pumpsey trotted over to the mound where Billy was digging at the dirt in front of the rubber with his shoe.

"Ground balls," Pumpsey said. "Ground balls and we got these suckers out of here."

It was the old motion and Dutch, trying to be careful not to watch too closely, felt relief wash over him. One batter at a time, he thought.

The first pitch was a ball and the next one came in like a fastball, but Darryl had called for the change-up and the batter took a cut long before the ball crossed the plate.

Hardcase pumped his fist in the air.

The next pitch was a curve and the batter got a piece of it, a slow ground ball to short. Pumpsey turned it to second and when it got to first Hardcase was stretched out. The double play ended the inning and Ava relaxed. Maybe it had been nothing. But Billy was usually the starter, not the closer, and she made a mental note to ask Dutch why there had been a change.

Billy pitched the ninth, three up and three down, and the Sox took a win into the late July night.

Chapter 15

Dutch Goltz agreed to leave his little house in Sacramento early and meet with Ava and Ray before Friday night's game. They were waiting in a corner booth in the Taqueria in Knight's Landing when he arrived.

"You want something to eat?" Ray asked as he sat down.

"If I eat something here, I'll pay for it all night long. I got nothing against what Maria makes, but I got an old kosher stomach that won't travel south of the border."

"Suit yourself," Ray said. "How about a beer?"

"That I can do," Dutch said.

"We need to do something about Bucky Collins," Ray said.

"You got anything in mind?" Dutch asked.

"I was thinking that Bucky needs to get visited by somebody who will remind him how painful it might be to screw around with us."

"Excuse me," Ava said. "Did I forget something? Or am I the owner of the ball club?"

"You are the owner," Ray said. "Nobody forgets that."

"So if you're talking about hurting somebody, you're including me in your plans?"

"You don't need to touch it," Ray said.

Ava slipped her hand inside the top of her blouse, running it back and forth on the flat plane of her chest, as if she were feeling for something. Perhaps her heartbeat.

"I don't want anything to do with some thug idea, Ray. You need to know that."

Dutch poured some of the Corona into his glass.

"Maybe we need to give Bucky a little cash and convince him that's all he's going to get. My guess is that a few hundred dollars will be enough to make him lay off," Dutch said.

"He'll drink that up in a week and be back," Ray said. "Billy closed out the game against Yuba City. He looked okay."

"He wasn't okay," Dutch said. "He was a single-A pitcher for five batters. But he wasn't the kind of pitcher he's been. And something needs to happen before he can cut his old man loose."

"You got any ideas?"

"Maybe." He looked across the table at Ava. "When I was a boy studying for my bar mitzvah," he said, "I was taught that a dog trained to attack Nazis was no more a good dog than a dog trained to attack Jews was a bad dog. Dogs can't reason. But people can. Compassion was a big word in those lessons. You don't want anybody to beat up Bucky Collins, even though he's a nasty drunk. I'd keep that in mind."

I'm beginning to sound like a rabbi, Dutch thought. Little stories for Billy and now Ava and what I really want to do is have somebody find that slimy little man and put him out of his misery. He poured the rest of the beer into his glass.

"You gonna pitch Billy tonight?" Ray asked.

"I'll use him as the closer," Dutch said. "Eight and nine. If we've got a cushion. We'll see how he does."

The Dog Sox had a two-run lead going into the eighth

inning. Dutch pitched Billy and he gave up one run. He wasn't the Billy Collins that Dutch wanted to see, but Darryl kept the pitches mixed and the curve ball worked.

He can't turn into a junk ball pitcher, Dutch said to himself. There's too much talent there. That's when he thought of Isaac and Aaron.

Chapter 16

Bucky Collins showed up at the Snack Shack in the third inning of Saturday afternoon's game. There he was, framed in the opening, waiting, with a grin on his face.

"Remember me?" he said to Ray.

Ray ignored him.

"Hey, asshole," Bucky said. "I want to talk to you."

"We have nothing to say," Ray said. "You can clear out now or you can wait while I call the sheriff and have a deputy clear you out."

"I paid my fucking four bucks, asshole. I got a right to be here."

"Last time I saw you, you threatened to burn the ballpark down. You went into the dugout and you had to be ejected. You're drunk. So get your ass out of here." Ray held out four dollar bills. "Here's your four bucks. Now clear out."

Bucky snatched the money

"I ain't through with you yet," he said.

"Nobody wants to see you. Your kid doesn't want to see you, I don't want to see you, the owner of this ball club doesn't want to see you. Go back to Humboldt County where you can drink yourself stupid and nobody gives a shit."

"I ain't in Humboldt County no more. I'm in Robbins and that ain't but twenty minutes up the road so you ain't seen the last of me. I ain't nobody to mess with."

"You got one minute to disappear," Ray said. "Then I call the sheriff. And you won't be in Robbins any more. You'll be a guest of Yolo County. And I'll make sure they stick it to you."

Bucky spat on the counter. "Fuck you," he said, as he turned his back and stumbled toward the gate.

Ray got the call from the Knight's landing fire department two nights later. He drove up the following morning to survey the damage. The Snack Shack was a pile of ashes and melted metal. There was a sizeable hole in the grandstand above the ruins. Jack sat in the passenger seat of Ray's truck and watched while Ray talked to Frank Gates, the volunteer fire department captain and liquor store owner.

"Somebody torched it," Frank said. "We could smell kerosene when we got here." He pointed across the parking lot toward the rice silos. "Night watchman saw the flames. It was going good when we got here. Lucky the whole place didn't go up."

"Did he see anybody?" Ray asked.

"No. Just saw the flames and gave us a call. You piss anybody off lately? Somebody who's a sore loser?"

"Maybe. You're sure it was torched?"

"No doubt about it. Smelled like kerosene or fuel oil and somebody poured it all around. Even burned the dirt." He pointed to black scorched earth that fingered out from the ashes.

"Somebody here in town who can fix those bleachers before Friday night?"

"Sam Donohue. Contractor."

"That's what I am. But I'm in San Francisco and I can't get anything done by Friday. You got his number?"

By Friday night the bleachers above where the Snack Shack had stood were repaired and the remains of the burned building had been carted off. It cost Ray seven hundred dollars. It should have been more, but Donohue said that he liked watching the baseball games and he had some down time and Ray was a contractor, too.

Maria's brother-in-law brought his Taco&Burrito Wagon to the ballpark. It was an old Winnebago with a fold-up side, decorated with gaudy paintings of tacos and burritos, and a gas plate inside where he turned out Mexican food for truck drivers and farm workers who stopped at the intersection of Highways 45 and 162 near Butte City.

Ray looked at the new planks on the bleachers and he remembered Bucky Collins' words: 'I'll burn your fucking ballpark to the ground.' I need some help with this, Ray thought.

Chapter 17

On Monday, Ray called Rocky Carbonera, who was his sheetrock sub-contractor. Rocky kept a crew of Portuguese men from the Canary Islands on call for big jobs and if Ray had an apartment house, like the one on Green Street, Rocky got it done quickly and within his estimate. There was never an over-run with Rocky.

Ray called him mid-morning.

"You got another job?" Rocky asked.

"Actually," Ray said, "I have a problem."

"Something wrong with the Green Street job?" Rocky asked

"No. It's something else. "You know how I bought that baseball team for the lady I go out with?"

"Fucking crazy," Rocky said.

"Yeah, I suppose it was. Anyway, I have this problem with a guy up in the Valley."

"What kind of a problem?"

"I've got a kid who's a pitcher and he's good. The problem is, he's got an asshole drunk father who's been showing up at the ballpark, and he's making threats against me, and the kid is falling apart. And last week somebody torched part of the ballpark and I think it might be this guy. So I was hoping that maybe you knew somebody who could talk to him."

There was a pause.

"By 'talk to him,' you mean convince him that it would be better for his health to disappear?"

"Something like that."

"What makes you think I would know somebody who could have this conversation for you?"

"People talk, Rocky."

"And if what they say makes sense?"

"I would discover that you underbid the Green Street job by a thousand dollars."

There was another pause, this one longer than the first one.

"Where would I find this guy?"

"He goes by the name of Bucky Collins. He's from somewhere up on the North Coast and my guess is that he's got a police record in Humboldt County. Maybe Yolo County, too. He says he lives in Robbins. That's a wide spot in the road about twenty miles north of Knight's Landing. That's all I know. "

"I'll look around for you, Ray."

Chapter 18

Friday night's game was with the Marysville Mudhens in their ballpark next to the lake in the center of town. It was a good park, and had, at one time, been the home of the double-A Marysville Giants, a farm team for the San Francisco Giants before the Foothill League folded.

Ray and Ava sat in seats behind the visitors dugout and watched Barney McChesney dig himself a hole in the second inning. He walked two batters, gave up a single, and that scored a run and left a man on third. A long fly ball scored another run and the next batter doubled.

Manny Garcia came in and hit the first batter, putting men on first and second. He wild-pitched the man on second to third and Dutch looked down the dugout at Billy. Billy looked out at the mound where Manny was fingering the rosin bag. Dutch held up his hands and called time.

He took his time getting to the mound where Manny waited, rolling the ball over in his hand.

"You think you can get two outs without too much more damage?" Dutch asked.

"You gonna pitch Billy?"

"Not if I can help it. We need two more innings. Then, maybe." Darryl had joined them.

"If you can throw down the pipe, keep them up, we can get out of this," Darryl said. "Nobody is going to dig in on you. They're afraid you'll drill somebody again."

"I might," Manny said.

"Nothing but smoke," Darryl said. "Don't try anything else."

"I ain't got much else," Manny replied.

Dutch looked at the scoreboard. "Let's just keep this respectable," he said.

Manny gave up two more runs and lasted until the sixth inning. Dutch pulled him and sent Billy in. Billy was good for an inning, then got shelled in the eighth and ninth and the Dog Sox lost, 12-2. After the game, Ray and Ava went to the Best Western Motel near the bridge that crossed the Feather River into Yuba City.

"Not a good night," he said to Ava when he came out of the shower. Jack curled up on the warm, damp bath mat.

"No," Ava said. "Win some, lose some."

"You okay?" he asked.

"Not really. I got a phone call yesterday."

"Who from?"

"Somebody who wanted to talk to you. Said he tried calling your cell but he couldn't get in touch with you so maybe I could give you a message."

"Who was it."

"His name was Rocky."

Ray waited. Ava said nothing more. She reached out and took the plastic glass with the ice and scotch and sipped it.

"What was the message?"

"That he hadn't been able to find the Bucky guy but not to

worry, he would take care of things."

She sipped again at the scotch.

"So what's he going to take care of, Ray?"

"It was a bad idea."

"You remember when I said to you that the only thing that would make me give you the gate would be if you were cruel?"

"I remember."

"I didn't mean cruel to me. I meant if I thought there was a cruel streak in you, I wouldn't want anything to do with you. You can be stupid or careless or a fuck-up, and it wouldn't matter. But cruelty. That's the line I wouldn't want you to cross."

"Bucky Collins beat up his wife and his kid and he tried to burn down the ballpark and he's fucked up his kid's life all over again and he's a useless drunk who doesn't give a shit about anybody except himself."

"Probably all of that is true, Ray. Remember what Dutch said about a dog that bites Nazis. It isn't necessarily a good dog. Beating up Bucky Collins, no matter what kind of a jerk he is, doesn't make it right."

"I said it was a bad idea."

She pointed with her glass to the open door to the bathroom. "Maybe you need to change places with Jack. I'm not sure I want you sleeping next to me."

"How can I fix this?"

"You tell Rocky you have second thoughts. You give me a week." She finished the scotch. "Maybe you could take me to Tiffany's again," she said. There was a hint of forgiveness in her voice.

Chapter 19

This is going to cost me, Ray thought. They entered Tiffany's and the stocky guard at the door smiled at them. Go ahead, smile, you motherfucker, Ray thought. I know what you're thinking. You're thinking that I'm some rich son-of-a-bitch or I wouldn't be with this beautiful woman and you make not much more than minimum wage to stand there and wait for somebody to make a break for the door with a fistful of diamonds in his hand, only the chance of that happening is in the same league as an earthquake dropping this building around our ankles. What you don't know is that I don't belong here but I'm crazy enough to fall in love with a woman who likes the smell of a place like this. And I won't get out of here without burns on my fingers.

Ava smiled at the clerk and said, "I would like to look at some necklaces. Perhaps an emerald pendant. Something simple."

Simple, Ray thought. Fucking simple. Simple minded is what I am, but he knew that he would not blink. The Green Street job, he thought. There's five grand profit in that one. And there was another job on Sansome that was an office remodel.

He could kite the Green street money onto the Sansome job and have maybe six grand left over. He watched Ava as she pointed to something in the glass case,

It was an emerald stone on a gold chain and when the clerk had draped it around her neck she turned to Ray, held her blouse open with her fingers so he could see the emerald glowing against her chest.

"Like it?" she said.

"It looks good," he replied.

"Good is not enough," she said. "You have to say it looks stunning. Or maybe that it lights a fire. Come on, Ray, if you don't want to change places with Jack, you need to be a bit more responsive."

The clerk smiled knowingly at Ray.

Hey buddy, Jack is a fucking dog, Ray said to himself. At least he thought he said it to himself.

"Gorgeous," he said

"Too late," Ava said. She reached up and undid the clasp, handing the pendant to the clerk.

"There," she said. She pointed to a tiny sterling silver heart that was shaped like a lock. "Put that on a chain,"

The clerk found a thin silver chain, threaded the locket onto it, and held it out.

"Yes," she said. "We'll take this." She lifted the chain around her neck and clasped it. The tiny heart lay flat against her chest.

Ray took out his credit card and paid for the locket. When they had stepped out onto Stockton Street, Ava turned to him.

"Did you think I was going to jack it up?"

"I had no idea what you were going to do. Guessing what your next move will be is like guessing the winning lottery numbers."

"Not funny," she said. "I wanted something from Tiffanys. But I didn't want to break the bank. And I've got some news for you."

They went to Campton Place where Ray ordered a French champagne and silently breathed a sigh of relief that he wasn't dropping the Green Street money on the Tiffany counter.

"So," he said, "what's the news?

"I bought a pitcher."

"You bought a what?" Ray had a momentary vision of something that was filled with water with lemon slices floating in it.

"A pitcher. A left-hander."

"When?"

"Monday. Dutch found him."

"Why didn't anybody tell me?"

"I'm telling you now. And you may remember that I'm the owner of the team. Right here." She placed her hand on the bar. "Somebody gave me the ownership papers. In this very spot."

"This lefty. Where did you find him?"

"You're not listening. Dutch found him. He's a high school teacher in Oroville. Manny knows him. He pitched in the Italian summer leagues for Milan two years out of college. He's in his thirties now and he plays some pickup ball, but Dutch said he's steady and he's what we need."

"Since when did you become the baseball wheeler-dealer?"

"Since I was a kid and I went to every A's game I could go to and my father played catch with me and taught me to throw overhand, and I'm not sure I like your tone. You think I don't know what I'm doing?"

"What did Dutch tell you?"

"That he wants to use Billy as a closer and Barney is good for about four innings so what he needs is a lefty who can be middle relief. This guy is big. He stands six-five and he's a sweetheart. You're going to love him."

"When do I see him?"

"Friday night."

"Is he expensive?"

"He's a high school English teacher who wants to play ball. Dutch worked out a deal. A hundred bucks for three innings."

"That's it?"

"And a free beer for every strikeout."

"So now do we go upstairs in this fancy hotel and have a meeting between the owner and the general manager?"

Ava fingered the silver locket at her neck. "Not unless the general manager apologizes for that remark about when did I become a baseball wheeler-dealer."

Chapter 20

Dutch met Isaac and Aaron at B'nai Israel synagogue in Sacramento on Friday mornings. A group of older men met to bake challah bread that was distributed to the homeless. Both men had worked in the diamond trade in New York, and the stories that they had shared during the Friday morning sessions when dough was rolled out and the loaves were shaped stuck with Dutch. They had grown up in a rough-and-tumble world where thieves were a constant threat, huge amounts of money could be at stake, and the police were never called.

"You can't take care of yourself, then you can't take care of anything else," Isaac was fond of saying. "I bake bread on Friday morning because I am atoning for things I did forty years ago. Things that were necessary, but they were not things I would tell the rabbi about. We knew people who would take care of problems for us. They weren't always kosher people. Sometimes you have to bend the rules a bit."

Aaron always nodded. He didn't say much, leaving the stories to Isaac. So Dutch asked them on the first Friday in August what they would do if they were faced with a Bucky Collins.

"This is a man who might drink himself to death?" Isaac asked.

"Maybe."

"So he should go to a bar and maybe he should have one too many and maybe he should get hit by a car or fall down some stairs, God forbid."

"That could happen."

"But it should happen soon and it would not be unusual if someone who became his friend should be there when he has his accident, God forbid that he should have an accident."

"I'm just wondering," Dutch said. "I was just thinking out loud."

"Maybe two old men might have a drink with your friend." He turned to Aaron. "You ever go out drinking with somebody and maybe he has an accident, God forbid?"

Aaron picked up a lump of dough and cut it into three parts. He rolled each part into a long strip, then braided the three parts into a challah loaf. He took a knife and cut another lump of dough into three parts.

"Once in New Jersey I heard about that happening," he said.

"If you find out where your new friend does his drinking, let us know," Isaac said. "That's what friends are for."

"Mostly in a little town called Robbins. I think there's only one bar there."

"Maybe we will drive up there for an afternoon glass of wine." He took Aaron's loaf and put it on a baking sheet with the other loaves. "It would feel like old times. God forbid that old times were better than the time we live in."

Aaron nodded assent.

Chapter 21

Barney started the game Friday night and the fact that Otis Bickford was on the bench seemed to give him an extra zip on the ball. Bickford was a hulking man, and Dutch had gone to some lengths to find a uniform that would fit him. But Barney knew that he only had to go four innings and then The Big O, as he was already called, would take over. Dutch sat down next to Otis.

"So you played ball in Italy?" he asked.

"Milan. Two years."

"Some good players?"

"There were some good ones. Probably single-A here."

"Any Italians?"

"Not many. They were mostly Americans, Puerto Ricans, Dominican. The manager was an old guy. Like you."

"Italian?"

"Alabama. Nobody could understand him. He couldn't speak Spanish so he couldn't talk to the Central Americans. He spoke some Italian, but his Alabama mushmouth meant that the Italians couldn't understand him. I spent a lot of time translating."

"You know Italian?

"I learned some. I already knew some Spanish. I grew up south of Market in San Francisco. Went to City College, played ball there before I got recruited at Arizona."

"You ever think you'd make it to the Bigs?"

"Maybe when I was in college. Not after, though."

"You have a good record in Italy?"

"I won more than I lost." He looked at Dutch carefully. "I'll give you three good innings, Dutch. And you'll owe me some beers. These guys" – He motioned to the batter that was facing Barney. He was down two strikes – "are not going to be a problem. I'm good for three innings. Then I wear out or they figure me out."

"That's all I need," Dutch said. "*Dos gefelt mir.* That's what my father used to say. Yiddish. It pleases me."

"You know that poem by William Carlos Williams about baseball? The one called 'The Crowd and the Ballgame'?"

"Not unless Williams stole it from the Torah."

"He's got a line in it. 'The Jew gets it straight,' he says. 'It is deadly, terrifying.' He's talking about the crowd."

Dutch looked back at the stands, then turned to Otis. "They don't look terrifying to me."

"He wrote that in the 1920's. Nobody up there is going to call you a kike tonight."

"Don't be too sure, young man." He watched as Barney fielded a weak grounder and threw to first. "You know a lot about poetry?"

"I teach English."

"I know men who coach baseball who don't know shit about the game. They know how to bat and field and sometimes they know something about pitching, but you ask them about somebody who did something in the 1920's and they'll have about as much clue as he does." Dutch pointed to the kid in the dog suit who had crept up next to Ava's chair. The kid waited until Ava petted him, then ripped off the head and sat up. Ava bent forward and kissed him on the forehead and the crowd cheered.

"Lucky kid," Otis said. "You got a looker for an owner."

"You met her boyfriend?"

"No."

"You make a move on her and you'll know him." The kid had the dog head on and was running on his hind legs toward third base. He dropped to all fours and rolled at the feet of the visiting team's third base coach. He got a kick in the ribs and the crowd booed.

"I'll remember that," Otis said. Barney had a full count on the batter and Dutch said, "Last of the fourth. Get warmed up. We'll see if you're as good as you say you are." He stood and raised his hand toward the plate umpire.

"Time!" he called and stepped out of the dugout toward the mound.

"Last out," Barney said. "I can get him."

"You got nobody on," Dutch said. "You got two outs. Drill him. Pitch him so far inside you get him in the ass. Next batter is going to be a little nervous. You'll have outs at second or first. You're fading." He looked over to the sidelines where Otis had thrown his first warmup. The smack as the pitch hit Manny's mitt was satisfying.

Chapter 22

The bartender in Robbins looked at the two old men who stood before him. They both wore polo shirts so they weren't Jehovah's witnesses. And they didn't look like bill collectors. They certainly didn't look like cops. They wanted to know if a young man named Bucky Collins came in regularly. Why these two sedate-looking old men wanted anything to do with a drunk like Collins didn't make sense. Maybe, he thought, they were from an insurance company. Bucky had been unable to keep his mouth shut about torching the ballpark in Knight's Landing.

"He comes in," the bartender said. "He ain't no young man," he added.

"Age is a relative thing," the taller one said. "You think he might come in this afternoon?"

"I doubt it."

"So maybe there is someplace else where he does his drinking?" the tall one asked.

"Maybe."

"So, he has a son who plays baseball. And we would like to discuss his son's prowess with him. So perhaps you would know where we could find the father of the baseball prodigy?"

"Butte City," the bartender said.

"So, this Butte City. Is it far from here?"

"Maybe forty-five minutes."

"And you are thinking that this Bucky fellow might be having a drink in this Butte City?"

"I am thinking that he got his sorry ass thrown out of here more or less permanently two nights ago. There ain't too many places left where he can still drink. Butte City is one of them."

"So, will it be difficult to find the place where he might be drinking in this Butte City?"

"Don't let the name throw you. One bar. Volunteer fire department. Two big farm sheds. A dozen houses. An empty gas station. Unless he missed the bridge and drove his car into the Sacramento River, you'll find him in the Butte City Club. Unless he's been eighty-sixed there, too."

The old iron bridge across the Sacramento River was anchored at the levee on the East end, and the road made a sudden left-hand curve down, passing a small pond that was ringed with trees. There were two huge farm sheds on the other side and just past the pond was the Butte City Club, a small square wooden building with peeling clapboard sides and two dark windows in the front with neon beer signs in them. One announced COORS, the other BUD. In between the signs was the door. There was a sagging screen on it and when Isaac and Aaron stepped inside, the darkness made it difficult for them to see anything. Two shadowy figures were hunched over the bar, and as Isaac's and Aaron's eyes adjusted, they could see that there were two men drinking and a portly bartender leaning against the back bar, watching them enter.

Isaac stepped to the bar and Aaron followed.

"What'll you have?" the bartender said, easing himself away from the back bar.

"We're looking for a young man named Bucky Collins," Isaac said.

The bartender turned toward the two men.

"Collins," he said. "You got company."

The man nearest them turned. "I ain't done nothing," he said.

Isaac approached him. "You have a son who pitches for a baseball team and is rather remarkable. So you must be quite proud of him."

"Are you guys scouts for a big league team?" Bucky asked.

"We are appreciators of the fine art of pitching a baseball," Isaac said. "We have watched the national pastime for many years. We saw Hank Greenberg in his heyday, didn't we Aaron."

"We did." Aaron said.

"I don't know no ball player named Greenberg," Bucky said.

"He refused to play on Yom Kippur in the middle of a pennant race," Isaac said. "They called him Hammering Hank."

"Never heard of him," Bucky said. "You here to talk about my kid?"

"We are here to buy you a congratulatory drink and discuss the exploits of your talented son."

Isaac motioned to the bartender. "Pour our new friend whatever he is drinking," he said, sliding a twenty-dollar bill across the bar. "And my old friend and I will each have a cold beer."

The bartender poured a shot of rye into a glass and set it in front of Bucky. He set a new beer next to the half-empty bottle on the bar and drew two drafts for Isaac and Aaron.

"You here to offer me some money for my kid?"

"Your son has a great talent."

"Who the fuck are you guys?" Bucky asked. "You got a funny way of talking."

"It is cloudy outside," Isaac said. "Which is not usual for this time of year in this place. Did you know that the prophet Shmuel produced the miracle of rain during the dry season when installing Shoul as King of Israel?"

"What the fuck are you talking about?" Bucky asked. He raised the glass and downed the shot of rye.

Isaac motioned to the bartender again. "Another one for my new friend," he said.

"I ain't never seen you before," Bucky said. "I don't know who the fuck you are."

"We are admirers of your son's talent," Isaac said. "God is interested, so to speak, in the justice of a father reaping the rewards of his son's success. No one should pluck the fruit from the tree and not acknowledge the labor of the tree."

"I still don't know what the fuck you're talking about," Bucky said.

"They treat you like a *nebbish*. A nobody, " Isaac said. "The man who manages the ball team is a *pisk malocheh*. A big talker. But we know how to deal with him."

"What do you get out of it?"

"I think you call it a piece of the action."

"Why the fuck should you get anything?"

"God forbid that I should presume to tell you how to live your life, but giving away a piece of something is far better than receiving nothing."

Isaac motioned to the bartender again. "My friend has run dry." The bartender poured another shot of rye and set a fresh beer next to Bucky. Isaac slid another twenty across the bar

It was dark when they left the Butte City Club. Isaac on

one side and Aaron on the other supported Bucky and they found his dilapidated pickup next to the road. They put him behind the wheel and watched while he fumbled for the key, started the engine and pulled out onto the road.

"Perhaps he will miss the bridge," Isaac said.

"Perhaps." Aaron said.

They watched while the truck climbed over the levee onto the bridge and disappeared down the two lane road.

"Perhaps he will have an accident," Isaac said,.

"I wouldn't count on it," Aaron said. "There are men who become *shnoshket* and can still steer their automobile."

"Perhaps he could drive into the river. God forbid he should miss the bridge, but that could happen."

"Once it happened in New Jersey," Aaron said. "The man drove off a pier and there was another young man who was a good swimmer with him. What we need is a young man who is a good swimmer."

"God forbid he should drown, but he does not seem to have many redeeming features."

"*Az mir fill schlugen a hunt, gifintmin a schtecken.* If you want to beat a dog, find a stick," Aaron replied.

Chapter 23

Friday morning Dutch went to the synagogue to make bread. The traffic on I-80 was thick and he was glad he didn't have to drive the commute every morning. Nearly every car had a single driver in it and they all had grim looks on their faces. I would move or quit my job, he thought, but he knew that in the Fall after the close of baseball season he would be in his truck on the freeway, driving to a job. Unless he could parlay Billy Collins into something that would give him a chance to escape. Maybe, if some team wanted Billy, he could hang onto Billy's tail, end up managing a farm club somewhere, or teach in a Dominican league baseball school.

Last Friday night's game had been satisfying. Barney carried a two-run lead to the bottom of the fourth and the new kid, the Big O, had done exactly what he had said he would do. He pitched three good innings, gave up three base hits, no runs, and the team owed him four beers. Fifteen batters and four K's. Billy closed and he seemed okay. His old man had not been back to the ballpark and Pumpsey said he hadn't been to the house in Woodland. He would ask Isaac and Aaron today if they had done anything. And if Billy got his stuff back, word would get out. A submarine closer, a real athletic freak. Dutch would handcuff himself to Billy Collins. *Ken zein*, he said out loud. Maybe. Could be. And he thought, shit, I'm sounding like my father. Is that what it means to be in your seventies? You start talking like somebody from another century. You become some old fart who rattles off Yiddish homilies and tells little stories and a glaze comes over people's eyes. He remembered his grandfather dimly. An old man with a white beard who always wore his yarmulke and could barely be understood. Dutch remembered being cuffed about the ears by the old man. "*Dumkop!*" the old man shouted. And he called Dutch *arunhoifer*. A street urchin. He had no tolerance for baseball.

Dutch liked the Bickford kid. Big. Handsome. Smart. And no illusions about some scout finding him on a Sunday afternoon in a rickety ballpark in a little Central Valley town and offering him a ticket to the majors. I must find that poem, Dutch thought. The only baseball poem I know is "Casey at the Bat." It's not too late to learn something new.

Isaac and Aaron were already in the synagogue kitchen when Dutch arrived. There were half a dozen men working at the table, and flour dusted the counters where loaves were being shaped.

"Sorry I'm late," Dutch said. "The traffic on 80 was terrible."

Isaac snorted. "This is not traffic. In New York it is traffic."

"And in New York everybody takes a cab," Dutch said.

Dutch washed his hands and joined the two men at the counter. They worked wordlessly for a few minutes and then Isaac said, "We have found your Bucky Collins."

"In Robbins?"

"He is no longer welcome in the town of Robbins. At least he is no longer welcome to drink there. We found him in a city named Butte."

"Butte? As in Butte. Montana?"

"No, as in Butte City. In California."

"You talked with him?"

Isaac placed the shaped loaf on the baking sheet. *Farshnoshket*," he said. "A drunkard. But he has an amazing capacity. And when we placed him in his automobile he could not stand but he was able to drive across a narrow bridge and not, God forbid, drive into the river."

"It would be nice if God did not forbid him to drive into the river." Dutch said.

"It was not an inexpensive conversation."

"I'll pay for his drinks," Dutch said.

"No," Isaac said, "We do this of our own free will. Aaron thinks he may have found the stick we can use to beat the dog with."

"What dog?" Dutch asked.

"It is a manner of speaking. Aaron remembers a similar situation many years ago when he lived in New Jersey. Perhaps it will be the answer to your predicament."

"Do I want to know what this stick is?" asked Dutch.

"No," Aaron said. "You do not want to know."

There was no more talk of Bucky Collins. Dutch left the synagogue two hours later, took the I-5 turnoff north and then onto 99. He was in Knight's Landing early enough to make sure the field was properly lined, that the lights worked and there were enough baseballs for the game. When Escobar Lopez pulled into the park in his Taco&Burrito wagon and began to set up, Dutch went over and bought a beer. He sat by himself in the dugout, looking out over the field. The late afternoon sun washed the grass and birds picked at the infield. Somewhere a dog barked. *Oy vey*, he thought. Two nice old grandfathers are plotting to end the life of a man and I'm on their side. I have become a dog that bites Nazis. Bucky Collins is a useless drunk and he's a pain in the ass and he could pound a spike into any chance that his son might have and, not so incidentally, my own greedy need to hang onto the kid's coattails. I have become a dog that bites someone because he's in the way.

Otis Bickford appeared at the end of the dugout.

"You're early," Dutch said.

"It's a nice afternoon," Otis said. He sat down, laid his glove on the bench, and opened a book.

"You do that often?" Dutch asked.

"Do what?"

"Bring a book to the ballpark. Read while you're on the bench. You did that in Milan?"

"Only until the game starts. Then I pay attention to batters. I keep a book."

"You keep a book on the batters?"

"They bat around in four innings. By then I know what they like, what they don't like."

"You write this book down?"

"I keep it in my head. I could give you the lead-off batter for Rome."

"A lot of young pitchers don't keep a book. They just throw what the catcher tells them to throw. All my life I've been telling them, if you don't keep a book, you'll never go anywhere."

Otis laughed. "If you've got a catcher who keeps a book, that works. But I can see things they don't see. How they hitch at their pants, where they look."

"What's that one?" Dutch asked, pointing to the book that lay open in Otis' lap.

"*Bang the Drum Slowly*. It' s an old one. I've read it before."

"He was a southpaw. Same as you."

"You've read it?"

"I saw the movie. Maybe thirty years ago. De Niro was just a kid. He played the dumb catcher. Played him right."

"You've got a good memory, Dutch."

"Are you suggesting that you're surprised an old man can remember a thirty-year-old movie?"

"No. A lot of people might remember the movie. But they wouldn't remember that De Niro got the catcher right."

"Anything that has to do with baseball, I remember. It's a curse. My head is full of shit. You tell me what the leadoff batter for Rome was a sucker for and I'll file it away. God knows why."

"We all have our curse, Dutch."

"And what would be yours?"

Otis laughed again "You give me another ten years and maybe I'll know. I think you have to live with it for a while to know what it is."

Smart young man, Dutch thought. He's a thinker. That may be his curse.

"So what's the story with the owner?" Otis asked. "How did she end up with this bunch of has-beens."

"Her boyfriend bought the club for her. For her birthday."

Otis raised his eyebrows. "No shit! He bought a baseball club and gave it to her for her birthday? That would be Ray, the guy who takes tickets and announces the line-up, right?"

"That's him."

"Is he loaded?

"No. As far as I know, he's a general contractor in The City and he's not loaded. She's a lawyer and I think she has more money than he does. But he calls himself the Dog Sox General Manager. Sort of the Billy Beane of the rice fields."

"He's the what?"

"General manager. She's the owner. I run the club."

"She know anything about baseball?"

"She's the one who okayed you. She's a sharp cookie."

"She's more than that."

Pumpsey and Darryl stepped into the end of the dugout and dropped their bat bags.

"Where's Billy?" Dutch asked.

"In the car," Pumpsey said. "Putting on his shoes." Pumpsey sat on the bench, took his baseball cleats out of his bat bag and began to unlace his street shoes. "Billy has a thing about not walking on a ball field in regular shoes," Pumpsey said.

Dutch turned back to Otis and lowered his voice. "You pitch three good innings," he said. "That's the deal. Fucking the owner isn't part of it. You need to remember that."

Otis looked down at the book in his lap. "I think that's in chapter three," he said. "Or maybe it was a different story. I'll have to look that one up."

Oy vey, Dutch said to himself. This is not what I need.

Otis looked up at him. "The leadoff batter for the Rome Gladiators always took the first pitch. So I gave him a big fastball, not much on it, right down the pipe. Strike one. He dug in for the next one, but I gave him a curve and he went for it, every time. And then, he sat back, waiting for that fastball again, and a couple of pitches later I gave it to him, only it was a change-up and the poor fucker either got air or he got a ground ball to short."

"I'll remember that," Dutch said, "whether I want to or not."

Chapter 24

When Otis started the fourth inning, the Dog Sox were down by a run. He set the visitors down, one-two-three, and in the bottom of the seventh Darryl punched a double, advanced on a single by Pumpsey, and scored on Manny's long fly ball to center.

Pumpsey, true to form, tagged up on the fly ball, barely beating the throw to second. Paul got a single to right, Pumpsey scored and the Dog Sox were on a roll. When Otis left the mound at the top of the sixth, they had a four-run lead.

"You're going to get a W if Billy holds up," Dutch said to him.

"I got four beers coming to me," Otis said. "Since I'm done for the night, I think I'll go collect two of them."

He went to the Taco&Burrito Wagon, took two Coronas and found a folding chair behind the dugout. He took the chair and the two beers to where Ava sat behind home plate.

"Mind if I join you?" he asked.

"Be my guest," she said.

He unfolded the chair, sat down, and held out one of the beers. She looked at the beer, then at him, took the beer from his hand and said, "I should be buying you a beer."

"You did," he said. "This is one of them."

"You did a nice job out there,"

"When I'm looking for the sign, if I look just a bit over Darryl's head, I can see you."

"Is that a distraction?"

"It is."

"You want me to move?"

"Absolutely not. Everybody thinks, he's having trouble getting the sign, but what's happening is that I'm thinking, I wonder if she would go out to dinner with me."

Ava tipped the beer up, then said, "Are you hitting on me?"

"Is that a baseball term?"

"You're pretty full of yourself, aren't you?"

"When I struck out that last batter I said to myself, Otis, what have you got to lose. The worst thing that can happen is that she'll tell you to take a hike and it's not like I'm paying the rent with this. You don't win the lottery if you don't buy a ticket."

"So you're waiting to see if you have a winning number?"

Otis was silent. In front of them Darryl was up again and the Mudhens had a new pitcher. "Man throws junk," Otis said, still watching the batter. "If Darryl waits him out, he'll get a hit." He turned to Ava. "Maybe I will, too."

"I've got a boyfriend. His name is Ray. Maybe you've met him."

"He's a nice guy. You live with him?"

"None of your business, handsome."

"Now that's a good sign"

"Don't get your hopes up."

"Hope is what it's all about. You hope the batter doesn't notice that your fastball isn't as fast as you'd like it to be. You hope the sun doesn't blind the centerfielder on that fly ball. You hope she'll say yes to dinner. Not here. In San Francisco. Good Italian restaurant. *Vorrei il piatto del giorno.*"

"Which means?"

"I'd like the dish of the day."

Ava didn't reply. She was looking past Otis at something, and when he turned, Ray was standing next to the chair.

"Dutch throw you out of the dugout?"

Otis held up the beer. "Can't drink one of these on the bench."

"You're in my chair," Ray said.

Otis rose. "I was trying to renegotiate my contract with the owner," he said. "Maybe get something besides a cold beer."

"Good luck on that one," Ray said. He sat down in the empty chair. Otis raised the bottle toward Ava. "Make me an offer," he said, and he turned.

"What the fuck was that all about?" Ray asked.

"Nothing."

"Bullshit. Was he coming on to you?"

"He's ten years younger than me, Ray. And I don't think he's the kind of guy who gives women ball clubs. Or buys expensive champagne." There was a crack! And the crowd erupted in a cheer, Darryl took a few steps toward first, paused to watch the ball sail over the left field fence, and then continued his trot around the bases.

Chapter 25

Dutch had watched Otis take the chair and the beers to where Ava sat. Not good, he thought. He may be my middle relief but he's getting to be a pain in the ass, and he could easily upset the apple cart. Apple cart. His grandfather had a cart, only it wasn't apples. It was rags and bottles; things that would be called recycles today. But the old man had collected, much to the embarrassment of the rest of the family, going house to house with his cart with the two high wheels. He piled bottles and cans in the back yard and once a month he called somebody who came in a pickup truck and hauled it all away and the old man flourished the bills, gave Dutch hell if he drank a Coke and didn't throw the empty bottle into the backyard pile.

Dutch looked out at the field where Paul was shagging a ball thrown across from right field by Pete Lubinski. That's what I'm doing, he thought. I'm gathering worn-out ball players and recycling them. I should get a big cart.

Billy started the inning with a strikeout and he looked good. He was ahead of the second batter when there was a commotion in the stands and a man came stumbling down the bleachers, lost his footing, and went face down behind the third base line. At first Dutch thought it was Bucky Collins. The man came unsteadily to his feet, a baseball cap jammed down around his ears and he waved off a man who tried to help him up. Shit! Dutch thought, but the man recovered, walked unsteadily toward the porta-potties and Dutch realized it wasn't Bucky.

But when he looked back at the mound, Billy was standing, watching the man enter the blue cubicle. The door shut and Billy continued to look. Darryl called to him, called time and went out to the mound. Dutch thought about joining them but when he stepped out of the dugout Darryl looked at him and shook his head. He said something to Billy and Billy nodded and Darryl went back behind the plate. The windup seemed the same, but the ball hung in front of the batter and he hit a line drive screamer back at the mound. Billy barely got out of the way and the ball was halfway to centerfield before it hit the ground.

The next batter got a single and Dutch realized he needed to stop the bleeding. He called time. As he started across the grass, Darryl stepped out from the plate, but Dutch waved him back. When he got to the mound, Billy was using his cleats to dig a hole in front of the rubber, staring down at the dirt, his right leg methodically working back and forth, not watching Dutch approach.

"Looks like you're pissed off again," Dutch said.

Billy stopped digging with his foot and began popping the ball into his mitt, looking at Darryl who stood talking to the plate umpire.

"That wasn't your old man who fell down on his way to taking a leak," Dutch said.

"I know that," Billy said.

"You ever drill anybody? Like maybe there was a pitcher

who threw at one of your teammates so the next inning when he came up to bat, you gave him a taste of his own medicine?"

"No."

"When I was a kid everybody told me that getting pissed off was a bad thing. It works against you. That's what my religion says, too. Don't get angry. Don't go for revenge."

The door to the port-a-potty opened and the drunk stumbled out.

"You want to take a shot at that poor son-of-a-bitch?" Dutch asked. "I'll bet you could nail him from here with a fastball. Put it right in his nuts."

"Why would I do that?"

"Just for the hell of it," Dutch said. "Let off a little steam."

Billy grinned. "Jesus, Dutch, that's crazy."

"Yeah, I guess it is. You got guys on first and third and no outs. Throw curves."

Dutch turned and went back to the dugout. *Oy vey*, he thought. I can't keep putting bandaids on this wound. It's full of pus and I need a way to lance it.

The batter stepped into the box and Dutch watched the windup. It was the familiar slingshot and the ball rose toward the plate and the batter took a cut. Nice curve, Dutch thought. Darryl looked at him and Dutch wiped his hand across his chest three times, touched his cap. Darryl crouched and gave Billy the sign and the ball that looked like it was coming in chest high on the inside went down and out. Maybe we'll get out of this, Dutch thought and the Big O will get his W. He looked again behind the backstop. Ray was sitting in the chair next to Ava.

Chapter 26

Ava got the telephone call at work. It was Otis Bickford and did she want to have lunch with him?

"What are you doing here?" she asked.

"Every once in a while I get fed up and I come down here where I can find book stores and a lunch that isn't a burrito or a burger. What I need is someone who would like to share a table at Sams in Tiburon with me. It's a table that looks out over the Bay."

He was waiting at the entrance when she arrived, towering over the others who were waiting for a table. When they were seated he asked," Would you like a glass of champagne?"

"Isn't that a bit rich for a school teacher's budget?"

"This is on the Dog Sox. I pitched two games last weekend. And you look like the kind of woman who drinks champagne for lunch."

When the champagne came, he raised his glass, touched it to hers and said, "So. What's the meaning of the name, Ava?"

"It means birdlike," she replied. "Like a bird."

"You don't look much like a bird," he said.

"Depends on the bird, doesn't it?

"Bird of Paradise?"

"Too gaudy."

"Some kind of a stalker. Heron. Egret."

"I'm not sure I like the sound of stalker. Are you an expert on birds?"

"No. But those birds have a grace to them, You have grace."

"I'm impressed."

"With my knowledge of birds?"

"No, I'm impressed with your line. Using a word like *grace* to describe a woman. What woman wouldn't like to hear that?" She took a sip from the champagne flute.

He pointed to a seagull that was standing on the railing on the other side of the window, looking in at them. "That's not you," he said. "That's a teenage seagull and it's been here since the sun was out and people sat out there on the deck and they threw french fries at it. And now the fog is in and we've got a dull, grey day and we're inside, only it can't figure out the glass part. We're behind a window but the bird is too dumb to know that. You'll notice that there aren't any adult seagulls around."

"How do you know it's a teenager?"

"It's brown. It will turn white when it matures."

"You ignored my question."

"I'm trying to think of a bird that's lithe. Sinuous. I'm still hung up on the egret. You see them in the rice fields up in the valley, these slender white things that look regal."

"What about Otis? What's the meaning of your name?"

"It means keen of hearing. Apparently my parents wanted me to listen. Also I had a great uncle named Otis who had a shitload of money. 'Be nice to Uncle Otis,' my mother used to say. 'He may be our ticket.' I was never sure what ticket he would buy for us. He left it all to the Rosicrucians."

"What are the Rosicrucians?"

"Weird religious sect. Uncle Otis was a mathematician. Strange man who thought science was the answer and the Rosicrucians had some things about healing that were tied to scientific thought. He was an oddball. My father couldn't stand him."

"Are you a good listener?"

"I pay attention."

"So pay attention now. No matter what kind of a bird you call me, you're not going to get a chance to fuck me. Is that clear?"

Otis looked out the window at the brown seagull. It cocked its head and looked quizzically back at him.

"I'm writing a book about the Dog Sox," he said.

"What's that got to do with it?"

"The moment I signed on with Dutch, I thought to myself, Otis, here's your chance. You can write the fucking novel that you've always wanted to write, and the characters are all there. Including this gorgeous owner who might be a sucker for a curve ball."

"Otis, you're not paying attention."

"I am paying attention. I just don't give up easily. In September I go back to teaching English to a bunch of cretins who bring very little to the table, but I keep at it, and sometimes it's like hammering nails into lead, but every once in a while a light bulb goes on over someones's head. So I keep at it."

"You're parked in a no-fucking zone."

"Maybe we'll move the car. You never know."

"Jesus, you're impossible," she said, "but it's hard to get pissed off at you."

She picked up the menu. "Time to order," she said. "I think

I'll get the carpaccio. Raw beef. Something really basic."

"Loon," he said. "Long neck, solitary, quite beautiful. Dark and mysterious."

"You're too much," she said.

"Take your time," Otis replied. "You'll figure me out eventually. You're a smart woman."

Chapter 27

"So," Isaac said, "you have found a stick to beat the dog with. Where did you find this stick?"

"I did an appraisal for him."

"You have been retired longer than I have. So, you are appraising diamonds again?"

"This was something different. A young man came to me with a special request. My nephew gave him my name."

"And what was this special request?"

"The diamonds belong to an old woman who is a friend of his grandmother. She has a new young friend who has told her he would like to buy them. She needs the money. But my nephew's friend thinks maybe she is being cheated. So he brings them to me. And he is right. There is one yellow diamond that is a stone beyond price. The young man is very grateful to me. And he is a good swimmer."

"God forbid that I should know what it is you have in mind."

"I am remembering something that happened a long time ago in New Jersey."

"If we do this thing, perhaps there will be a *shlok*. A curse on us."

"If we do this thing, perhaps we repair a life. We have done enough in our lives to deserve the *shlok*. We are two old men who have seen enough to know when to take a stick to an ugly dog."

Jimmy Ferris left his car behind the sheds opposite the Butte City Club. He found Bucky Collins at the bar, half-way hammered, and it only took him a few minutes to strike up a conversation. Within another fifteen minutes, he was Bucky's new best friend, mostly because Jimmy bought the drinks. But Jimmy was careful to stay sober and when they left the bar, Bucky was staggering.

He is so shitfaced, Jimmy thought, that this will be a piece of cake. They found Bucky's pickup. Bucky had some trouble opening the door and even more trouble getting into the seat. When he was behind the steering wheel and had fumbled the keys out of his pocket, Jimmy said, "Hey, pardner. Let me have those keys. There's no way you can drive this fucker."

"I can drive better drunk than you can drive sober," Bucky muttered.

Jimmy reached out, took the keys from Bucky's hand and pushed him into the passenger side. Bucky was dead weight and it took some pushing, but when he was far enough over, Jimmy slid behind the steering wheel, put the key in the ignition, and started the engine.

Bucky sagged against the window.

"You know where I live?" he asked.

"Absolutely," Jimmy replied. "You are home free." But Bucky didn't hear him. He had passed out.

Jimmy opened the door, turned and took off his shoes. He stuck his wallet inside one of them, his watch inside the other, and carried them to the base of a tree next to the highway. Then he went back into the idling truck. Bucky hadn't moved. He pulled onto the highway toward the bridge, but immediately turned off , driving on the gravel parallel to the levee until he found a maintenance road that angled up. When he got to the top he stopped, looked down to where the river rolled slowly, a black presence in the headlights, and he turned the steering wheel. There were several lights on the bridge downstream and the reflection of the water below the black outline glistened. He touched the accelerator and the pickup dipped over the edge of the levee. It was a gentle slope down and Jimmy pressed hard on the brakes, so that the truck went slowly toward the water, the tires breaking free in the dirt and brush, and when the pickup entered the river, Jimmy opened the door on his side, slipped out and began to stroke toward the bank.

The truck went quietly under the surface, huge bubbles gurgling up as it disappeared.

Shit, Jimmy thought. I've fucking killed a man. And he climbed out onto the levee, scrambling up the bank on all fours. Behind him there was no sign of the pickup. Oh shit.

A few minutes later he found his shoes, put them on over his wet socks, crossed the highway to the shed and slid into his car, dripping wet. He was shivering and he turned the heater on full blast. He turned out onto the highway and drove toward the bridge. Suddenly he saw him, right there, in the headlights: the drenched figure of Bucky Collins, unsteadily staggering toward the road. "Fuck!" Jimmy said out loud. "The son-of-a-bitch is alive!" He thought for a moment that he would aim his car at the stumbling man, but then he was driving up onto the bridge and Bucky was a dim apparition in his rear view mirror, stumbling across the road toward the Butte City Club.

Chapter 28

Saturday afternoon's game with the Red Bluff Rangers was a home game and it was a scorcher. Barney started off hot, retired the first three batters, two on weak grounders and one with a strikeout. By the bottom of the third inning, everybody in the dugout recognized that Barney was going one-two-three. Nine batters, nine outs, and the Dog Sox were up by three runs. But more importantly, Barney was pitching perfect no-hit ball. In the fourth inning Barney began to lose it. He walked the first two men, then hit the next guy to load the bases. Dutch went out to the mound while Otis got up to throw his warm-ups at Manny along the first base line.

"I can do this, Dutch," Barney said. "I got one of *them* going."

Dutch looked at him. "I know I'm not supposed to say the word or it's a jinx, Barney. You've got a three-inning no-hitter going only you've got no outs and the bags loaded." Darryl had joined them, holding his mask in one hand. Dutch turned to him. "What do you think?"

"Sorry Barney," Darryl said. "You left your stuff in the dugout after last inning."

"Come on," Barney said. "You guys don't understand."

"What I understand is," said Dutch, "that you pitched three great innings and now we're going to bring Big O in and if he keeps it going and Billy closes it out we'll get a win. And I'll buy you dinner for three perfect innings." He reached out his hand, palm up. Barney placed the ball in it and waited while Dutch turned and waved to Otis who trotted toward them.

Otis finished out the inning with a force at the plate and a throw back to first that doubled the batter. A strikeout and the inning was over.

By the time the sixth inning was finished, Otis hadn't allowed a hit, and he came off the field easily. "No problem with me, Dutch," he said. "You owe me four beers."

Billy started the seventh with a no-hitter in progress. Of course it wasn't the same as a single pitcher going the full nine without giving up a hit, but Otis sat back and announced to the bench. "Nobody say the fucking word. The kid does it and Barney and I and the kid can all say we pitched one of them. We just don't have to say how much we pitched."

"It doesn't count if three guys do it," Paul said,

Otis leaned forward, looked down the bench and said, "It fucking does count. And it's going to be a chapter in my book."

"What book?" Manny asked.

"The book I'm writing about you dog butts. You're all going to be famous."

"Bullshit," Manny said. "You ain't no Stephen King."

"Stephen King doesn't write books about baseball," Otis said. "So shut up and give the kid some help."

Billy was on his second batter, and he looked good. Apparently his drunken father had receded and Darryl's sign was all he seemed to care about.

"Way to go, Billy!" Otis shouted. "This guy's a sucker for a curve ball."

The batter looked at the Sox dugout, grinned, and dug in a bit deeper. He never saw the fastball.

Chapter 29

Ray turned the lights on in the ninth inning and Billy was unhittable. It was like watching a strange, athletic dancer on the mound, who stood, motionless, and then rose up, only to dip and thrust forward in a motion that was both violent and graceful, and the ball was a white blur and Dutch knew that he was watching something special.

When the game was over the crowd drifted off into the gathering darkness, the lights went on in cars in the parking lot. The team packed their bat bags and left, slapping each other on the back. Ray checked to make sure the equipment shed was locked. He found the switch for the field lights, flipped it, and the floodlights began to fade. They glowed red for an instant before the park went dark.

"Just you and me, babe," he said to Ava.

"I got us a couple of beers," she said, touching the cold glass of one of them to his cheek.

When they got to the car, Jack jumped into the back seat. Ava closed the door and said, "Let's walk to the river."

It was still warm and the rice bugs and mosquitoes hummed. They went toward the lights of the bridge that crossed the Sacramento, and went up onto it. The occasional car came up the incline and crossed, the tires buzzing on the grated metal surface. Below them the river was black and oily. It seemed still.

"It's hardly moving," she said.

"That's where you're wrong," Ray said. "It's a lot of water. Maybe thirty yards wide here and it's deep. It's a big volume and if you were to fall in, it would sweep you along."

Ava bent and picked up a chunk of wood that lay against the rail. She dropped it over the side and they watched as it went downstream at a steady rate.

"I could swim that fast," she said.

"You could swim with it but you couldn't swim against it. Or across it," Ray said.

"I'm a good swimmer. I could swim across. I'd go downstream some, but I could do that."

"No," Ray said. "You can't do it. So don't even talk about it."

She turned and started toward the far side of the bridge. A truck labored onto the bridge and passed close to them, and when Ray called out to her she didn't turn her head. He caught up with her and said, "Where are you going?"

"I could swim back from the other side," she said. She pointed downstream to where the rice silos were silhouetted in the night security lights. "I would come out right about there."

"No," Ray said. "It's a fucking stupid idea." He reached out and took her am and held her. She pulled sharply, breaking free.

"You don't think I can do it, do you?"

"It doesn't matter what I think. It's black and it's powerful and you could die."

"You wouldn't dive in after me?"

"If I dove in *I* would drown. That much I know."

They had reached the far side of the bridge and she stepped

off into the dirt, turning toward the river bank that sloped down to the water. She held out the beer bottle to him. "Here," she said. "Hang onto this." She unbuttoned her blouse, slipped it off and held it out.

"This is insane," Ray said "What's the point? okay, yes, I believe you can do it. Is that what you want to hear? Now put that back on and we go back across the bridge."

Ava folded the blouse. She stepped out of her sandals, placed the blouse neatly on top of them, unbuttoned her jeans and, raising first one leg and then the other, stepped out of them. She folded them and placed them on top of the blouse.

"Jesus Christ," Ray said. "What's got into you?" A truck came across the bridge and Ava, standing in her bra and panties, was momentarily caught in the headlights. The driver blasted the air horn twice.

Ray reached out toward her but Ava stepped down the incline just out of touch.

"You can't stop me, Ray," she said. She turned and stepped down into the water.

"No!" Ray shouted but she knelt and slipped into the water. Almost immediately she began to move downstream. She began to swim, powerful strokes, her legs churning the water into a white froth in the bridge lights and then she was another ten yards downstream, disappearing in the blackness. Ray bent, grabbed her clothes and sprinted back across the bridge. He came off the other side running, stumbling in the hot darkness toward the rice silos. When he came into the halo of light in the graveled parking lot he turned toward the river. The blackened limbs of the burned eucalyptus trees towered over him. He stopped at the river bank and shouted her name and kept shouting and then, miraculously, he saw her emerging a few yards downstream, stumbling up through the blackened brush, holding onto it as she came into the light. Ray ran to her, pulled her up and enfolded her in his arms, pulling her tight against his body.

"Where's my beer?" she finally said.

"I don't have it." he replied.

"Shit!" She said. "You lost my fucking beer?"

"Jesus, Ava, I'm sorry. I'll buy you a whole goddam brewery."

"You bought me a whole goddam baseball team, sweetheart."

When they got to the motel and were inside unit #6 she shed her wet panties and bra and went into the bathroom. Ray listened to the shower run for a long time and finally he opened the door. The small room was filled with steam and he said, "You okay?"

"I am now," she said. "It was fucking cold!"

Ray looked back at Jack, who lay at the foot of the bed.

"You have no idea," he said to the dog, "no idea at all. You just think whatever we do is what human beings do and all you want is a scratch behind the ears and something in your dish." He picked up the wet panties and bra and laid them over the back of the chair.

Ray poured a scotch for himself, another for Ava, and sat on the edge of the bed, listening to the shower. When it stopped, he stood, waiting for the door to the bathroom to open. Ava came out, still rubbing the towel through her hair , her skin pink from the hot water, and Ray said, "Are you okay?"

"Yes," she said. She tossed the towel onto the chair, crossed the room and pulled herself to him.

"What was that all about?" Ray asked.

"I don't want to talk," she said. "I want you to fuck me. I want you to pretend you just met me for the first time and I want you to find every part of my body, and I want to lose myself in you."

She unbuttoned Ray's shirt and pressed herself to his chest and she pulled his hand down to touch her and she pressed harder against him. "Things we've never done before," she said. "I want it to be something you won't find in any book." She pushed him back onto the bed and climbed onto him, rising until she was poised over his face. "I want you to split me in half," she said. "Find the core of me."

Ray had no idea what time it was. He lay, filled with lassitude. He could only remember that it had been more than he had ever imagined anything could be, and now, they were no more than empty husks, and they were silent, next to each other, and he could hear her breathing and he thought that perhaps she was asleep.

He touched her thigh gently, felt the silky smoothness of her skin. Ava spoke, in not much more than a whisper, so softly he could barely hear her voice.

"I watched those three guys this afternoon. They were so intense and it seemed like nothing else mattered to them. And I thought, what have I got in this world that matters that much to me."

"It was just a ball game," Ray said.

"No. Barney pitched three perfect innings and Otis came in and he just overpowered them, and then there was Billy, It was like he was from some other planet and I wanted to feel that way."

"So you swam the river."

"Yes," she said. "You said I couldn't do it and suddenly I had to."

"You scared the shit out of me."

"When I was in the middle, and I was caught in the flow, I

was scared. It pulled at me and it was black and the rest of the world was shut off. I thought I wouldn't see you again. I could see the lights and I could hear you shouting my name and the river was pulling at me and I was so cold."

"I cannot imagine losing you. Don't pull a stunt like that again."

"I'm not planning to."

"You didn't plan this one."

"No, it came over me. It felt like I was on fire."

"You weren't on fire when you came out of the river. You were more like ice."

"Fire and ice. That's what it felt like."

"How do you feel now?"

She reached over and touched his lips with her fingers. "I think we put out the fire," she said. "And we melted the ice. We probably could have melted a glacier." She laughed softly.

"I won't do that again," she said.

"Which? Swim the river or what comes after?"

"Swim the river. Everything else is still on the table."

Chapter 30

When Billy came into the dugout he looked hangdog and beat-up, and he slumped onto the bench. Dutch noticed that he had his street shoes on.

Dutch motioned to Pumpsey and they stepped out of the dugout, down the first base line.

"What's with Billy?" Dutch asked.

"He's hung over."

Dutch looked back at the dugout where Billy was sitting in his stocking feet, not moving.

"Hung over? You guys had a party?"

"Not exactly. Billy doesn't drink much. Maybe a beer now and then. But something weird happened and he got shitfaced. Darryl and me had to cart him home before he got hurt."

"Was this in Woodland?"

"No. We don't go out much in Woodland. You ever see any black folks in Woodland?"

"I wouldn't know."

"How many black folks you see here in Knight's Landing?"

"You. Maybe a few when teams come from Yuba City or Marysville. Fans who live up there."

"So I don't do much in Woodland except sleep in a rented house with Darryl and Billy and eat at MacDonalds. Maybe Jack-in-the Box sometimes. I want to find a girl to dance with I got to go to Oakland or Vallejo or Richmond. Yesterday Billy says he wants to go with me. Which means that he's gonna be the white face in a dark room."

"So you took him with you?"

"I told him he was gonna be the odd man out. But he said he wanted to go. So I asked Darryl to go along. I figured we might need some bulk if things didn't work out. Not that I expected them not to."

"Do they call you names over there in Woodland?"

"No. Nobody does that. But I know better than to drink in a bar and ask some white girl to dance. You wouldn't know about that, though."

"You haven't been a Jew-boy who had to be careful which girl he asked to dance."

"You don't wear that all over your skin."

"Maybe not, but when I was your age, it felt like it."

"When you were my age was a long time ago."

"So what happened last night?"

"We went to a club in Vallejo, mostly black folks, some others, so Billy and Darryl weren't too conspicuous. Billy had a couple of beers. He's not much with the girls and he's kinda geeky-looking so he kept pretty much to himself."

"Billy is not twenty-one. How could he drink in a club?"

"They weren't too particular about carding anybody. They know me."

"So Billy wasn't exactly the life of the party?"

"No. He's pretty much a loner."

"But you did okay."

"I found a hot mama and I was thinking maybe Billy and

Darryl could go back to Woodland on their own and I could get a ride back today, but then some guy began dissing his girl, calling her names, said she was acting like a whore, and Billy, he got all pissed off and told this guy to knock it off. Which was not a good idea."

"So what happened?"

"Billy told him he ought to go pick on somebody with a dick but maybe that would be too much to ask, and Darryl and me had to hustle him out of there before he got creamed."

"So you came back to Woodland?"

"No, we went to another club but Billy kept it up, began drinking shots and beer and he got shitfaced and he wanted to go back to the first club and beat the shit out of that guy and Darryl and I had to get him home. Fucked up my night, that's for sure."

Dutch looked again at the dugout. Billy hadn't moved, was still sitting with his stocking feet in the dirt.

"His old man show up lately?"

"No. You think he's got something to do with it?"

"Yeah, I think so." Dutch put a hand on Pumpsey's shoulder. "Thanks for keeping an eye on him."

"No sweat. But he sure ain't going clubbing with me again."

Dutch went back to the dugout where Billy was finally putting on his cleats.

"So," Dutch said, sitting down beside him. "You had a big night, did you?"

"Nothing special," Billy said.

"You going to be okay by the seventh inning?"

Billy looked up. His voice was defiant. "Why wouldn't I be?"

"You look a bit fragile."

Billy yanked at his shoelaces and one of them broke. "Shit!"

he said. He took off the shoe and began splicing the broken ends together.

"Get a new shoelace," Dutch said.

"I don't have one."

"Borrow one from one of the guys. Take one out of your street shoes. Never go out on the field with a bandaid on your equipment."

Billy looked at him. "Maybe you should take one out of your shoes and loan it to me," he said. "You're not going to pitch today."

Oy vey, Dutch thought. I need to find the magic words to calm the Golem. Before it eats its own arm.

Chapter 31

Ray kept Fridays open because the Dog Sox always played on Friday nights. He and Ava had fallen into a routine in which they spent Thursday nights together in her loft south of Market, then drove to Knight's Landing, and came back Sunday after the third game. The Central Valley League played three games a week, Friday night, late Saturday afternoon, and Sunday. It was a forty-eight game season and now, in mid-August, the Dog Sox were leading the league with a 25-13 record and Ava was showing a profit.

Ray got up early Friday morning and stood at the sliding glass doors that looked out toward the Bay Bridge. Behind him Ava slept, one arm thrust out, her hair a wild explosion about her head, and Ray began to examine the fantasy that occurred to him whenever he stood at the door. He imagined that they were in a small hotel somewhere in Italy, or perhaps Morocco, looking out over the Mediterranean. The door opened to sand and nothing else, only the blue of the sky and the sea that lapped on the shore not far away. He imagined Ava standing in the doorway. Her red hair was a halo around her skull, and she faced the sea, and she wore only a white shirt, one of his, that she had put on after she had come out of the shower. It was hot, suffocatingly hot, and she stood there, looking out toward the water, and he was consumed with desire for her. He knew that, despite the shower, her skin would have a sheen of sweat and it would glisten and he would want to touch her, slide his fingers over her breasts, down over her belly, feel the silk of her skin. The sun was sinking into the sea and they waited for the green flash, but it did not come. There was only the last redness and then it was gray and he said, we should eat, and she said. Not yet. Not until it is so dark I cannot see you, only know that you are there by touch. And he knew again why he loved her.

He turned back to where she was stirring awake.

"You standing there waiting for somebody?" she asked.

"No, I was thinking of us taking a trip."

"To where?"

"Maybe Italy. I've never been to Italy. You have. You speak some Italian. You could be my translator."

She rolled over, pulled the blanket up to her chin and patted the bed next to her.

"What do you want translated?"

"How about, 'You look really beautiful when you first wake up'?"

"Ray, I look terrible. My face is puffy, my hair is a mess, you have no standards at all. How can I believe you?"

"So what's the Italian?"

"*Sembri molto bella.*" She laughed. "Why don't you just say, Ava, it's the same old story. Or maybe just let me guess."

Ray reached over to run his fingers through her hair. "When I was a kid you could buy a kit that had a drawing and there were numbers and if you could count you could paint the picture. Four was burnt umber and six was blue for the sky and when you were done if you squinted your eyes it looked a bit like Andy Warhol or maybe Peter Max."

"I don't remember Peter Max," Ava said, "but you're much older than I am. So what's the point of this stroll down memory lane?"

"I'm not that much older than you are," Ray said. "From now on," he added, "we'll use numbers. One is for fucking beautiful. So all I have to do is look at you and say 'one'."

"And two?" Ava asked.

"Two is sporty, wide awake, your green eyes, laughter men would kill for. Three, is elegant and tailored. Four is a night at the symphony, a silk dress and street lights on wet pavement and holding my breath because maybe you will disappear at the intermission, like Cinderellla and I'll have to spend the rest of my life calling out 'Four! Four!'"

"You are fucking crazy," she said.

"Five is early morning, in a hotel in Morocco, white shirt, no makeup, holding a chipped mug of coffee in both hands, listening to the sound of the sea. Or maybe it's in the Alps and it's the sound of a river. Only it's a river you're not allowed to swim."

"Is there a six?" She asked.

"Now we go into other areas," he said.

"Such as?"

"Six is a Manhattan. You want a Manhattan, all you have to do is say 'six.' Seven is calamari and eight is Veuve Cliquot champagne. Nine is the bar at Campton Place. The one where we drank champagne and I gave you the Dog Sox."

"I think we did more than drink champagne at that hotel."

"We'll call that ten."

"That's calamari. That's what you like. There must be a number for something I like. Prosciutto?"

"Eleven. And, right now you look a brilliant five."

She pulled the blanket down so that she lay naked and said, "Is there a number for this?"

"It's part of being a five." He reached out to run his hand over the smoothness of her belly.

"I forgot. What's a five?"

"White shirt, coffee, sea. Morocco."

"I was never very good at math," she said.

"This isn't math. This is shorthand. It's like remembering the telephone number of a man you're in love with. That ever happen to you?"

"It was a number in Rome."

"Jesus," he said. "I'll bet you remember the number of his apartment."

"Is this a test?" she asked.

"No."

"Good," she replied. "Is there a number for an omelette and coffee?"

"Try ten," he said.

Chapter 32

Billy didn't show Friday afternoon at the ballpark. Dutch watched Darryl and Pumpsey drop their bat bags in the dugout and, when Billy didn't turn up, he asked Darryl where he was.

"I don't know, Dutch."

"He didn't come with you guys?"

"He's been gone two days."

"What do you mean, he's been gone two days?"

"Just that. He left in that old beater car of his on Wednesday and we thought he was going to the store or something and he never came back. Not Wednesday night or Thursday either."

"Nobody called me!"

"We kept thinking he would show up. I thought he'd be here. He's never missed a game."

"You never called the police or a hospital or anything? You never called me?"

"Dutch, he's a big boy. What was I going to say? One of my roommates took off and he didn't say where he was going?"

"Pumpsey said he had trouble when he went out with you guys last week."

"He was drunk that night, Dutch. "

"He didn't say anything? Where he was going? Has he got a girlfriend?"

"Dutch, it doesn't say anything in my contract about babysitting Billy. If he's got problems, they're his problems, not mine."

Oy gevalt, Dutch thought. What was it has grandfather had called it? *A kappore.* A catastrophe.

When Otis went on into the eighth inning, Ava knew something was up. Billy wasn't on the bench and Otis didn't look happy. He took his time between pitches, fingered the rosin bag, threw to first in what wasn't a pickoff move, just a casual throw. Then came an inside pitch that dusted the batter off and something that looked like a spitter that Darryl had trouble handling.

Ray came over with two beers and sat next to her.

"Where's Billy?" she asked.

"Nobody knows," Ray said.

"What do you mean, nobody knows?"

"Just that. He disappeared on Wednesday and nobody's seen him since."

"You think he's quit on us?"

"Dutch thinks it has to do with his old man."

"The drunk?"

"That's the one." Ray tipped his beer up. Another pitch went off Darryl's mitt into the dirt.

"I think our boy is throwing illegal stuff," Ray said. "But he's good enough to hide it so the ump can't call him on it yet."

"What makes you think that?"

"Darryl keeps dropping pitches, and that isn't like him. And the ump keeps asking to look at the ball."

"You mean Otis is being a naughty boy?"

"I mean Otis wants to survive out there and he's gone one

inning more than he usually goes."

"What do we do about Billy?"

"Not much we can do. Wait to see if he surfaces."

But Ava wasn't content to wait. Otis survived another inning and Manny closed, giving up two runs, but the Sox had a four-run cushion, so Otis got the W. After the game, as the team gathered their jackets and bags, Ava showed up in the dugout. She motioned to Pumpsey.

"Take a walk with me," she said.

They walked along the first base line toward the outfield. Insects clouded the light poles.

"You got any idea where Billy is?" she asked.

"I told Dutch. No. Not a clue."

"He ever go off by himself like this?"

"No."

"Has he got a girlfriend?"

"Not Billy. There's a girl in Maria's Taqueria that he likes. Mexican girl. He hung around there. But her brother told Billy if he laid a finger on his sister, he'd do something."

"Like what?"

Pumpsey looked uncomfortable.

"Spit it out," Ava said.

"He said he'd cut Billy's dick off."

"That might make you think twice," Ava said.

Chapter 33

The next morning, Ray and Jack took off for The City in his truck and Ava stayed behind. She told Ray she was in no hurry, didn't have to be back at work until afternoon. Midmorning she went to Maria's Taqueria and found the girl.

"You know Billy Collins?" she asked.

The girl was making tortillas for her uncle's Burrito and Taco Wagon.

"*Sí.*" One syllable. She didn't look up.

"He's missing. Went someplace and hasn't been back for several days. You have any idea where he is?"

"No."

"Is he afraid of your brother? Your brother have anything to do with his disappearance?"

The girl looked up. "No."

"Does that mean no, he's not afraid of your brother or no, your brother isn't mixed up in it?"

"It means no."

"Do you know who I am?"

"You're the señora who owns the *beisball* team."

"So if I'm looking for Billy, I have his best interests at heart, right?"

"Billy said he was going to see his mother."

"Billy's mother is dead."

"*Si.*" The girl stopped pressing the tortillas. "He says he is going to go see her and I tell him, your mother *es muerte.* Dead. And he says, he knows that."

"You think he was going to do something to himself? "

"*No se.* I don't know."

"So, where do you think he went?"

"I don't know. He drove off. My brother says good riddance. He says Billy is crazy."

"We're all a little crazy, sweetheart."

A phone call to the *Fortuna Record* told Ava that Mabel Collins had died two years earlier of cancer and was buried in the only cemetery in Fortuna. Ava debated calling the Fortuna police, She looked at her watch. Two hours up Interstate 5 to 36, another hour west across the mountains to Fortuna. She could be there by early afternoon. If it turned out to be a dead end, she could come back down 101 and be home by evening. We're all a little crazy, she had told Rosa Lopez. Maybe I get the prize.

It was two o'clock when she found the cemetery, a grassy knoll that hung over the Eel River. And there, parked among the headstones, was a beatup Chevrolet Camaro. Somebody was slumped in the front seat.

Ava parked and went toward the car, careful to stay in front of it so whoever was sitting inside would see her. She didn't want any surprises.

It was Billy Collins.

He stared straight ahead when she got to the window.

"Billy," she said. "Roll down the window."

He didn't move.

"Come on, Billy, don't be difficult."

She went around to the passenger side, opened the door and slid into the car.

"You been here long?" she asked.

"At night I slept in a friend's house."

"What are you doing here?"

"I don't know."

"Which one is your mother?"

Billy pointed to a small flat marker next to the car.

"I watched her die," he said. "In the end I had to dress her. Take her to the bathroom. She had scars on her body, places where my old man busted her up. Now that son-of-a-bitch has showed up again. I thought I was shed of him for good."

"What do you want, Billy?"

"I want him to die. Like she did. Just waste away."

"You want anything else?"

"Like what?"

"I'm just trying to figure out what's going through your head. You want to play baseball in the majors?"

"That would be good. But I don't think it's going to happen."

"Why not?"

"Sometimes I have it and sometimes I don't."

"Have what?"

"There's times when I throw the ball and I know exactly where it's going. I could throw it at a hole in a board no bigger than a baseball and it would go through without touching anything. When I was a little kid I used to line up soda cans on a fence and practice knocking them off. And there's other times when the ball leaves my hand and I just hope it goes where I want it. There's times it feels like it's dynamite and it freaking explodes and there's other times when it's just a baseball. Nobody pitches in the Bigs when it floats like that."

"So your old man shows up and you lose your stuff."

"Don't ask me why. All I can see is him beating on my mom and I can smell that kitchen and his stink and I wish that I was nobody. That he couldn't find me ever again."

"You want to play catch with me?"

Billy looked at her. "What do you mean?"

"Just that. Get a couple of mitts and a baseball and play catch. You pitch to me."

Billy smiled. "You want me to pitch to you?"

"Why not? Just throw me a few pitches. See if I can handle them."

"You any good?"

"My father used to play catch with me. He was pretty good."

"Bucky never played catch with me. Once he came to see me pitch when I was at Fortuna High. He was drunk and they had to call the cops."

"If I said I had two mitts and a couple of baseballs in my car, would you throw a few pitches at me?"

"How did you know I was here?" he asked.

"Rosa Lopez said you were going to see your mother. I took a chance."

"It's hard to figure you out. You sit behind home plate with a beer and you're really good looking, I mean you're a knockout and you know baseball, and I don't think you take any shit off anybody. I never knew a woman like you."

"There's probably some others like me out there."

"Did you know that the kid in the dog suit has the hots for you? And that Otis wants to get you into bed?"

"That's not news to me."

"Will Otis get you into bed?"

"Do you think I sleep around, Billy?"

"You and Ray seem pretty tight. I don't think so. It's not that you're not a good-looking lady. But I don't think of you that way."

"I know that. I never thought your head worked that way. I'm sorry I asked that question."

Ava opened the door of the Camaro and stepped onto the worn grass. She crossed to her car, popped the trunk and took out two mitts, two baseballs, and tossed them, one at a time, to Billy, who stood next to the Camaro. She tossed him a mitt and walked past the headstones to an avenue of grass and turned to face him.

"No heat," she said. "Just change-ups."

Billy took a soft windup and threw the ball to her. She fielded it easily.

"Throw harder," she said. "I'm not made of glass."

The next pitch had a bit on it, and Ava took it with ease and Billy laughed. "Hey!" He called out. "You're not bad for a girl."

"I'm going to ignore that," she said. "That 'for a girl' shit. Throw the fucking ball and put something on it."

The next pitch slammed into her mitt with an explosive whack! and she said, "That's more like it."

Billy waited while she threw the ball back.

"This time," Ava said, "I want you to throw it at that." She pointed to a headstone that had a small figure of an angel on it. "See if you can nail it. Right on the nose."

Billy hesitated, then went into his windup and the ball sped toward the headstone, hit the angel in the nose and bounced off.

"Not bad," Ava said. She retrieved the ball and tossed it back to him.

"This time," she said, "I want you to imagine that it's your old man. The asshole. He shows up and you say to yourself, fuck off, you drunk old man, and you wind up and you give him your best shot. "

"Did you ever play baseball?" Billy asked.

"No. I played some softball, but they didn't let girls play with the big boys. I think that's where I got my edge. You know what that is?"

Billy nodded.

"So, can you throw one of those pitches, the one where you know exactly where it's going?"

Billy stood for a moment, looking at the headstone.

Come on, Ava said to herself. Do it! Billy reached back with one foot, as if he were touching the rubber, and he went into his windup. The ball was a blur when it came out of his hand and hit the headstone with such force that it split the seams and bounced off, the core rebounding through the grave markers, the cover falling at the base of the angel.

"I think, Billy Collins," Ava said, "that you need to get laid. Find that girl in the Taqueria and tell her you think she's a number one. And when she says, what's a number one, you tell her, it's the number for beautiful. One is beautiful and two is full of life and three is just plain who gives a fuck about your brother!"

"Rosa doesn't like me to use words like that."

"Then find another word. But keep the one and the two." Ava held up the mitt. "One more," she said. "Right in here."

Billy bent, picked up the other baseball.

"You want me to put something on it?"

"You think I can't handle it?"

He grinned, went into his windup. Ava held the mitt steady, and the ball hit the pocket with enough force to burn her hand, driving her backwards. She held up the ball, turned, and threw it across the cemetery toward the river.

"That's it," she said. "Let's you and me go have a beer."

"Does Ray know you're here?" Billy asked.

"I do what I want," Ava said. "Ray is important to me, but he doesn't own me. Your old man doesn't own you either, Billy. You throw the ball through the hole or you don't. It's up to you."

"Why did you come up here?" Billy asked. "You afraid I wouldn't pitch and you'd lose the rest of the games?"

"I like winning, Billy. More than most. But that had nothing to do with it. My guess was that you were in a lot of pain and everybody was sitting on their asses waiting to see what would happen. I just wanted you to know that you weren't alone in this mess."

"You ever have anybody beat on you when you were a kid?"

"No. I was luckier than you. But I had something else. If you grow up with nice tits and a pretty face, people tend not to give you your due. They think that's all you are. A pretty face and nice tits. I'm a lawyer, Billy. Men see me coming and they think, 'Terrific, I'm up against an airhead.' Sometimes I think it would be easier if I were flat-chested and had a plain face. But I don't. So I kick their asses." She looked across the cemetery toward the river. "It's like throwing a baseball through a hole in a board. It feels good."

She started toward her car. "Let's get that beer," she said.

Chapter 34

The buzzer rang and Ava hesitated before answering it. She expected no one. Ray had gone to San Jose to bid on a job, and it was too late for the office to call. She pressed the button and asked, "Who is it?"

"Your middle relief," came the voice. It was Otis.

"Are you lost?" she asked.

"I have an unerring sense of direction," the voice said. "I am like a homing pigeon."

"This isn't your roost," she said.

"I brought you something."

"Some kind of a message tied to your leg?"

"It's a copy of Bob Feller's *Strikeout Story.* 1947. Mint condition. I found it in a used bookstore and I opened it and immediately I knew you had to have it."

"And why would I have to have that book?"

"Because you're the owner of a baseball team, you like baseball and on page twenty-two he describes his first big-league game and the manager says he'll pitch the middle three innings.

Which is what I pitch for you, and I said to myself, this is too good not to share with Ava."

"So now we're on a first name basis?"

"It foggy out here," Otis said. "Any chance I can come up and give you this book?"

Ava hesitated again. Why not, she thought. She pressed the buzzer and waited until there was a knock at the door. She opened it and he stood there, a boyish grin on his face. He held out a book with a green cover, slightly worn on the edges.

"Bob Feller," he said. ""Seventeen years old and a big league pitcher. Not that different from our Billy."

"You came all the way here to give me a book?" she said. She stepped back and Otis came into the room.

"Nice," he said, looking around. "Pretty much what I expected. Elegant. Clean lines. Classy. Pretty much matches the occupant."

"Clever line, bozo. You didn't come all the way here to give me a book, that much I'm sure of."

"I am cut to the quick," he said, still grinning.

"How did you find out where I live?"

"A bit of detective work. You own a baseball club. It's part of the Valley League. The Valley League has a secretary in Sacramento who, for the price of a lunch and the vague promise of a dinner found the papers that show you're the owner. And here I am."

"And some poor girl in Sacramento thinks you're going to take her out to dinner?"

"I made no promises."

"I'll bet that's a recurring theme in your life."

"Ouch!" he said. "You wouldn't happen to have a beer would you? It's like a desert out there."

"I thought you said it was foggy."

"A foggy desert."

Ava went to the refrigerator and took out two bottles of Trout Slayer beer. She popped the caps, and brought them back to where Otis was now sitting, leaning back on the couch, his legs crossed.

"Make yourself at home," she said, handing him the beer.

"Is that one of those things you say that's just a formality or are you offering an invitation?"

"Jesus," she said. "You are so fucking full of yourself. You are good-looking, you're smart, and you think you're God's gift to the world. I don't know whether to laugh or just throw your ass out of here right now!"

"Please laugh. You have one of those laughs that men kill for."

"I've heard *that* line before," she said. She reached out for the book, and sat down on the couch. She opened the book, and began to read, "Feller pitches today and I'm going to bear down on him. It's time I stopped babying these guys." She turned to Otis. "This is supposed to turn me on? Is that the idea?"

"I thought you might like to read it. He was one of a kind. You are, too."

"You're writing a book about the Dog Sox, right? What am I, Otis? Chapter twenty-three? The one where the middle relief guy bangs the owner?"

"I haven't gotten to chapter twenty-three yet."

"So what am I? Something you hope to chalk up in the win column? Along with the secretary in Sacramento?"

"I wouldn't chalk you up as a win. More like a no-hitter. Feller pitched a no-hitter. They come once in a lifetime."

Ava closed the book. He smiled, as if he were waiting for an answer to a question. She held the book out and he took it, placing it on the table next to the couch.

"What is it you expect?" she said.

"I'm not sure," he replied. "Perhaps you can tell me."

"That's a new one." She picked up his beer, took a sip and put the bottle back on the table. Then she added, "If I said, 'Take me to dinner,' where would you take me?"

"Il Correra in North Beach. The chef is from Veneto in Northern Italy. If you go to Veneto, you have to know Italian. Nobody speaks English."

"And you've been there?"

"I played baseball there."

"You're a man of many talents."

"Come to dinner with me," he said.

"You get dinner," she replied. "That's it. We're not at chapter twenty-three yet."

"I'll remember that."

Why am I doing this? Ava thought as she pulled her sweater on over her head. Otis was waiting at the door for her, his hand on the knob.

"Remember," she said, "you're parked in a no-fucking zone."

"How much is a ticket?" he asked.

She suddenly remembered the threat Rosa's brother had made toward Billy.

"They cut off your dick," she said.

Chapter 35

When Dutch picked up the phone he was surprised to hear Pumpsey's voice.

"Billy's back," he said.

"With you guys?"

"He came back this morning."

"Is he okay?"

"Depends on what you mean by okay," Pumpsey said. ""Right now he's out in the back yard pitching at beer cans."

"What's that supposed to mean?"

"He's got about twenty empty beer cans lined up against the fence, on a board that's just about knee high, and he's throwing baseballs at them."

"How's he doing?"

"He's fucking nailing them. I never seen nothing like it, Dutch. Here." Pumpsey held the phone up. There was a sound like a shot, and a pause, and then another one.

"That's him, Dutch."

"Is he going to show up for the game?"

"That's what he says. He says he wants to start."

"Did he say where he was?"

"No."

"I would ask you to put a leash on him and make sure he gets to the ballpark, but that's probably not a good idea."

"You want to talk to him?"

Dutch could hear the pulsing shots behind Pumpsey's voice.

"No. It sounds like he's got some kind of a rhythm going. Just make sure he knows when to stop."

Chapter 36

Through the window Ray could see her sitting at the bar, waiting for him. She had a flute of champagne in front of her and he stood for a moment, watching. Her sweater was grey. It was a vee-neck sweater, and its soft curves clung to her body. A silver necklace glowed dully at her neck, and it was matched by earrings that were tiny silver eardrops. Her glasses had darkened slightly in the sun, and when she turned her head he was struck by the intensity of her look, as if she had important news or was about to let him in on a secret. Her skirt was black, as were her stockings, and she crossed her legs, turning from the bar so that the light from the street caught her cheek and her hair, and he imagined her in a courtroom, the jury listening as she read something to them, pausing to let the words sink in. They would pay attention to her, he thought. They would hang on every word. She was black and grey and silver and pale skin at the base of her throat, a tinge of red in her short-cropped hair. It wasn't just that she was beautiful. There was something that shone from her, some inner sense of rightness. Now she reached for the flute and sipped at the drink and the word that came to him was *grace.*

"How long were you standing there?" she asked when he sat down on the bar stool next to her. The bartender appeared and asked what he would have.

"One of those," he said, pointing at her glass.

"How long?" she repeated.

"Not long. I didn't know you could see me."

"And what were you thinking?"

"Just admiring you."

"I found Billy Collins yesterday," she said.

"Dutch called me. He told me he was back in Woodland. Where did you find him?"

"In a cemetery in Fortuna. Next to a marker with his mother's name on it."

"I'm not going to ask how you found him. It's a long goddamn way to Fortuna."

"The kid needed to be found. Nobody was looking for him. Not you or Dutch or the guys he lives with. Everybody just waited, hoping he'd come back up to the surface."

"But you didn't wait."

"No."

"There's something else going on here, isn't there?"

"Probably." The bartender set the drink in front of Ray and he touched it to Ava's glass. "Here's to you," he said.

"Who am I, Ray?"

"I'm not sure I understand the question."

"Am I just an attractive woman, someone with nice tits who likes dogs and baseball? Who, exactly, do you think I am?"

"Aside from the fact that you can't pass a dog without saying hello to it?"

"Aside from that."

"You remember that morning in the kitchen of your loft when I came to bid the job?"

"Yes."

"There was something about you that made me want to do that project more than anything. I wanted to please you. I didn't job out the cabinets to a cabinet maker. I made them myself. I borrowed the shop from Rocky and I did what I hadn't done in years. I put them together, piece by piece, and I made sure they were perfect. Because I wanted to please you. I wanted you to open those cabinets in the early morning and you would touch them, and part of me would be there when you did that."

"That's about you, Ray. What about me? If I were to disappear, what would you miss?"

"Am I a friendly witness here or a hostile witness?"

"No jokes, Ray. I was in the car by myself yesterday for ten hours. I had a lot of time to think."

"I never gave anybody a baseball team before. Not even close. I never reached down to pull a wet woman out of a river at night and I never told my secrets to anyone else before."

"You haven't told me all of them."

"No, but more than I've ever told anyone else. You're one of a kind."

"Sort of like Billy Collins."

"In a way. He pitches. Lots of guys pitch a baseball. But he adds something to it that nobody has ever seen before. You could say he's a freak or you could say he's one of a kind. Either way, he's unique. So are you. I can't predict what you're going to do next. I like that. I'm never sure that you know what you're going to do next. But I sure as hell love you for it."

He touched his glass to hers again. "That's about as good as I can do."

"It's good enough," she said.

Chapter 37

When Dutch gave Otis the nod at the top of the fourth, he trotted out to the mound with a comfortable 4-2 lead. He touched the rosin bag, turned to face the plate, and Darryl crouched for the first warm-up. Just beyond Darryl's head was the chair where Otis expected to see Ava, but there was someone else in the chair. It was a young woman who looked vaguely familiar and when Darryl threw back after the pitch, Otis let the ball drop so that it rolled off the front of the mound toward the plate. He went forward, bent to retrieve it and as he stood, he got a better look at the person sitting in Ava's chair. It was the pretty secretary from the league office in Sacramento and she smiled at him, raising her hand in a tiny wave.

Holy shit, Otis thought. He looked around for Ava, but there was no sight of her. Otis tried to remember the girl's name. What the fuck was she doing here on a Friday night and what was she doing in Ava's chair, and the first pitch he threw to a batter went over Darryl's head into the backstop.

Settle down, he told himself. The girl had long blonde hair and she was wearing a tee shirt and a baseball cap. It was a Dog Sox cap with the little black lab just above the bill and Otis counted to ten. Darryl gave him the sign a second time, and he threw a fastball that went where it was supposed to go but the batter connected sharply and the ball went into short left. Not a good start, Otis thought. Not a good start at all.

He bore down after that, and retired the side, striking out the left fielder who had never gotten a hit off Otis. He ended the inning with a curve ball to the shortstop who hit a weak grounder that Pumpsey turned into a double play.

Back in the dugout he thought about talking to the girl but then he thought better of it.

"You okay out there?" Darryl asked.

"Yeah, I'm okay. I just needed a few pitches to settle down."

"You see that babe sitting in the owner's chair behind the plate?"

"How could I miss her?"

"Sweet," Darryl said. "Maybe she's related to Ava. A niece or something."

"Could be," Otis said.

When the top of the sixth ended, Otis trotted off the field with the Sox still ahead by one run. "You owe me two beers," he said to Dutch. "I'm going to collect them now," and he left the dugout. But he didn't go to the Burrito wagon. He went to the chair behind home plate. As he approached, she smiled and said, "You were great! Really great!"

"Not as good as I usually am," Otis replied. "And it's a surprise to see you here."

"It was supposed to be a surprise. Ava called me and said you wanted me to see you pitch and she was coming up for the game and she would pick me up in Sacramento and give me a ride. She said you'd give me a ride back after the game. Is that okay?"

"Absolutely," Otis said. What the fuck is her name, he asked himself again. Her blonde hair was pulled through the back of the baseball cap into a pony tail and the tee shirt was a Dog Sox tee shirt, tight enough to emphasize her shape.

"Ava gave these to me," she said, pointing to the tee shirt and cap. "She's over there," and the girl pointed toward the dugout.

He turned, and there, standing at the end, were Ray and Ava. Ray was intent on Darryl, who was at bat, but Ava was watching the two of them. She raised her hand and pointed her index finger at Otis. Then she traced in the air the letter K, the symbol in a scorekeeper's book for a strikeout.

Otis turned back to the girl. No point in striking out twice, he thought. "What you need," he said, "is a Dog Sox uniform shirt with your name on the back. Remind me how you spell your name."

Chapter 38

Darryl waited out the first two pitches and then Ray watched as he dug in, squared against the pitcher, the bat poised above his shoulder. It's perfect, he thought. The field was dark green under the lights that had turned on after the fifth inning, and there was a hum in the air. It was a mixture of the voices from the stands, infield chatter from the players, the highway beyond the left field, and the insects that filled the air, and Ray thought, yes, this is the kind of moment when everything else disappears and all I can think of is the batter and the pitcher and what must happen next. The pitcher bent, fingered the rosin bag, stood, facing Darryl. He dipped, intent on the catcher's sign. Darryl swung the bat over his shoulder again, and then everything stopped, and Darryl and the catcher and the plate umpire were like statues and the pitcher wound up and it seemed to Ray that it was all in slow motion. When the ball was released it was difficult to see, it came so fast, and Darryl swung and there was the sound that Ray remembered from his boyhood, the impact of wood against the speeding ball and then the world came into motion again, fielders moving, Darryl running, the second baseman scooping the ball and throwing without coming erect, the ball and Darryl arriving at first base an instant apart.

He turned to Ava and put his arm around her and drew her against his body.

"What's this all about?" she said.

"A base hit."

"A base hit turns you on? You're a funny guy, Ray Adams."

"That's what's charming about me," he said. He pulled her tighter against him and as Pumpsey entered the batter's box he realized he no longer cared about the game.

Chapter 39

Dutch watched Billy wind up and deliver, and he thought, Billy needs to straighten out his landing foot. He's off balance and a shot drilled back at the mound would catch him unable to fend it off. But, Dutch thought, maybe I don't want to mess around with what's going on out there. I could upset the delicate balance of things and destroy the beauty of it.

The ball came back from Darryl and Billy fingered it, rolling it in his hand. The batter squared against him waving his bat menacingly over his head, but Dutch knew that inside the batter's head things were swimming in syrup. The pitch would come and he would wait it out or swing blindly, but he wouldn't have a clue where it would cross the plate.

Billy leaned forward, then rocked back and his arm came up in an arc that seemed impossible, as if his shoulder and the upper half of his body had become part of the arm, and when he bent forward, the arm swept down, his knuckles just above the dirt and he released it and Dutch thought, *Oy vey*, I have never seen anything like this. This is a boy who has invented something so startling that I cannot tell anyone about it. There are no words to match what I am seeing.

As Billy wound up again, Dutch imagined him on the mound in a big league park. I would be sitting on the bench in the dugout, he thought, He will be the discovery that takes me to the Show one last time. The ball popped in Darryl's mitt and the batter tapped the plate twice with the bat, turned and started back toward the visiting team dugout.

Fantazyor, Dutch thought, I have become an old man who builds castles in the air.

Chapter 40

Billy stopped the car a hundred yards short of the taqueria. It was dark along the road and he waited. Several trucks passed, rocking the car in their wake and then he saw the solitary figure approaching. She passed the taqueria and came toward his car and he reached across to open the door on the passenger side. It swung open and Rosa slid in next to him. She said nothing.

"It's cold," Billy said. He started the engine, turned on the heater and waited.

"My mother will be here soon," she said. She pointed through the windshield toward the sky. "That's the tortilla star," she said.

He looked up. A single star was caught just above the crescent of the moon.

"I never heard it called that."

"We call it that," she said. "It's the star that women see when they get up to make the tortillas."

"Will you get in trouble meeting me like this?"

"If anybody finds out. My brother is still sleeping. So is my father. This is the time women get up."

"I'm glad you came," he said.

"Did you see your mother?" she asked. "When you went to the cemetery?"

"I saw her marker."

"In Mexico we celebrate *Dia de los Muertos*. The Day of the Dead. We honor the dead ones, bring food and drink to where they lie. It is the first day of November that we do this."

"Are you from Mexico?"

"I was born here. In Knight's Landing. But my mother and father are from Mexico. And I have been there."

"You bring food to the cemetery?"

"We bring the favorite things that they liked when they were alive."

"My mother liked chocolate cake."

"I could bake a chocolate cake for you to take to her grave."

"Maybe you could come with me."

"I would like that," she said.

"I've never had a girlfriend," Billy said. His voice was hesitant.

"I have never had a boyfriend," she replied.

Chapter 41

She wore a white shirt, open at the neck, and a slender necklace of garnets, blood drops against her pale skin. She was, Ray thought, the beginning of a story about a woman who stands at the edge of a baseball field. It was dusk and the sun slanted through the trees. She held a chipped coffee mug in both hands and looked through the trees to where the river flowed, dark green now, and listened. He could not tell what she was listening for, but it seemed as if she were listening for something more than the traffic on the unseen road and the wind sighing in the trees. Her figure was white against the green and gold and yellow. Ray remembered a painting in the museum that she had admired. It was a woman standing in a field, a French peasant woman whose sheep were not far behind her. When he had bent close to the painting he saw that the woman's body was not much more than a few strokes where the brush had touched the canvas. There were a few swirls, like white mud that formed her breasts and what he had thought were birds were no more than drops of blood among the grass at the water's edge. And now Ava stood at the edge of a field like the woman in the painting and Ray waited at the edge of the dugout, afraid to touch the moment, afraid that if he moved or spoke it would dissolve.

He remembered another time when he had been mesmerized like this but he could not remember if it was her sharp intake of breath or his that froze the moment in his head. Words had been whispered that were knitted together into this story, forming a garment that would keep out the demons. Threads of ivory and grey and persimmon were threaded into stripes and a fabric that fit so close to her skin it had become part of her

She touched her fingers to the necklace, drew back her hair with one hand and laughed. The sun had gone behind the trees now, and there were lights spilling from houses and she turned to face him.

"You waiting for something?" she asked.

"Just watching," he said.

She came toward him and he realized that she was barefoot.

"You notice who was in the burrito wagon tonight?" she asked.

"Not really. Lopez was there, but he's always there."

"Rosa Lopez. The niece."

"Is there something significant about that?"

"She's Billy's new girlfriend. He asked her to come and see him pitch."

"How come you know this?"

"I'm the owner. I make it a point to know what my ballplayers are up to."

Ray laughed. "I doubt if George Steinbrenner cares who Jason Giambi is going out with."

"This is Billy the Kid, we're talking about. Billy the Innocent. Our submarine whiz kid. The only problem is, if Rosa's brother finds out, he may break Billy's arm."

"Why?"

"Because he's a *gringo* and Rosa is sixteen and nobody is

going to touch her unless the men in her family approve and Billy is a long way from the approved list. "

"Why not? He's a nice kid."

"You know that and I know that, but he's outside the circle."

"If Rosa's brother breaks his arm, I'll break the brother's neck."

"We need to stay out of this, Ray. Let Billy work it out. It's new territory for him, and I think he'll tread lightly."

"Is that what you were thinking out there on the field?"

"Among other things." She looked down at her bare feet. "The grass feels good. You ought to take off your shoes and try it."

Chapter 42

When Dutch arrived at the synagogue on Friday morning, Isaac and Aaron were already there, braiding challah loaves.

"You have troubles with the traffic again?" Isaac asked.

"It gets worse every time," Dutch replied, washing his hands.

"Transporting from one place to another is not easy here," Isaac said. "In New York there are trains. Trains above and trains below. Here everyone is in an automobile."

"Not everyone," Aaron said.

"Which reminds me," Isaac said, "Has your Mister Bucky been to see you lately."

"Not for a while." Dutch paused. "Did something happen to him?"

"Yes and no," Isaac said.,

"Sometimes," Aaron added, "the dog is stubborn and you need to find a bigger stick."

"What does that mean?" Dutch said.

"*Er drayt sich arum vie a furtz in russell,*" Isaac said.

"You lost me there," Dutch said.

"He wanders around like a fart in a barrel. He is not easy to catch."

"I thought you found him in a bar in Butte City."

"We did. Patience is a virtue, Dutch."

"So you're looking for a bigger stick. Is that it?"

"This will be perhaps the best bread we have made," Isaac said. "It is soft like a woman's breast and it will rise like the moon."

Obviously, Dutch thought, the subject has changed. He watched the two old men shaping challahs, twisting the dough into braids and placing them on a baking sheet.

They were not brothers, but they seemed joined at the hip. He had never seen one without the other. He wondered what their lives had been like on the Lower East side of New York. Isaac was the talker. Aaron was the mostly silent one. But Dutch had the feeling that it was Aaron who made things happen. Aaron would be the one looking for a bigger stick.

Chapter 43

Otis lived in a tiny apartment in an old house along the levee in Oroville, reached by a stairway that had been scabbed onto the outside wall when they converted the second floor into a separate unit. He could look out over the Feather River from the big double-hung windows that were above the desk where he wrote and corrected student papers and sometimes sat with a scotch and watched the egrets that nested in the trees along the river lift off at dusk. They settled along the banks and became white exclamation points that, if you didn't know they were egrets, could have been mistaken for sun-bleached sticks .

Otis had just poured himself a scotch when he heard footsteps coming up the stairs. There was a knock and when he opened the door he was surprised to see Pumpsey and Darryl standing on the small landing.

"You guys lost?" Otis said. "Woodland is a fucking long way from here."

"We have a problem," Pumpsey said.

"Who is 'we'?" Otis asked.

"Us. The Dog Sox."

Otis stepped back and Pumpsey and Darryl stepped into

the room.

"You guys want a beer? Scotch? Something?"

"A beer would be nice," Darryl said.

"Yeah," Pumpsey echoed. "A beer would be nice."

Otis took two beers out of the little refrigerator and twisted off the caps.

"So what's the problem?" he asked.

"Billy."

"Billy's old man?"

"No, something else," Pumpsey said.

"What else?"

"Billy has a girlfriend."

"That's a problem? Sounds more like an answer."

"It's who she is. She's the niece of Lopez, the burrito wagon guy. Her mother is Maria, who runs the Taqueria in Knights Landing."

"And why is that a problem?"

"Because her brother heard about Billy hitting on her and he thinks Billy is fucking her and he's going to get some of his buddies and kick the shit out of Billy. I mean really clean his clock. Break some things."

Otis took a sip of his scotch. He looked out the window at the river and then back at Pumpsey and Darryl who were standing self-consciously in the middle of the room.

"Where do I figure in this?" Otis asked.

"We need to find the brother and convince him that if he lays a hand on Billy he will suffer serious damage."

"You need to back up, Pumpsey, and run at this again. I'm not sure where I fit into this little soap opera."

"Billy is just a kid. The girl is sixteen and we're pretty sure he's not banging her, right Darryl?" Darryl nodded. "You're big. What are you, six-four? Six-five? And you weigh maybe 230 and

Darryl here is built like a Hummer and I been around. I know how to handle myself. So we thought maybe the three of us and Manny Garcia could find this brother and convince him that Billy isn't worth getting the shit beat out of him."

"Sort of a vigilante committee, right?"

"For Christ's sake, Otis, the kid is part of the team."

"I get a hundred bucks and a few beers for three innings on Friday and another hundred on Saturday, Pumpsey. I barely know you guys. I've been teaching here three years and I know the kind of guy that brother is. I know what it's like to get a new idea into a hardhead like that. Talk to Billy. Tell him to find a girl who isn't under lock and key."

"We talked to him. You're not going to believe this, but she's going to bake him a chocolate cake on the first of November and the two of them are going to drive to Fortuna on the coast and put it on his mother's grave."

Otis took another sip of his scotch. "*Dia de los Muertes*," he said. "Fucking crazy." He paused, then added, "Not the Day of the Dead. Taking the girl to Fortuna, that's what's crazy. What does our boy use for brains?"

"You're not going to help?" Pumpsey asked.

"Help you do what? Corner some rockhead who wants to beat up somebody he thinks is banging his sister? And then do what? Beat him up? Invite the whole gang of them to the ballpark for hot dogs and a beer afterwards?"

"You're an asshole, Otis."

"Obviously Billy never asked you to do this."

"He doesn't know we're here. Manny knows. He said yes."

"To what? Is he going to put on his cop uniform and bring his gun and cuff the poor bastard, arrest him for conspiracy to protect his sister?"

"Somebody is going to beat the shit out of Billy. Darryl and

I live with him, sit on the bench with him, he wins games for us. We need to find the brother and talk to him, but we need some bulk. And we thought you were a good guy. That's why we came here. Maybe it was a bad idea."

Otis turned to look out the window again. Shit! he thought. I don't want to do this. He remembered the season he had played single-A ball in West Texas. The ballparks were scruffy, the grass brown, and every once in a while there would be a nest of fire ants. The groundskeepers poured gas into the nest and torched it. Put a stick in there and they swarmed all over. He remembered that. And they were vicious. This wasn't much different, only they couldn't pour gas on Rosa's brother and get rid of him.

He turned to face Pumpsey and Darryl.

"If I go along with this, there have to be some rules," he said.

"Like what?"

"We don't just beat him up. That won't work."

"So what do we do?" Darryl said. "Talk him to death?"

"You're smarter than that," Otis replied. "What's better? Trying to overpower a batter, or getting him to go for the sucker pitch?"

"Depends on the sucker pitch."

"Exactly. You want Rosa's brother to change his mind? You offer him what he wants. Or at least that's what it looks like you're offering him."

"This isn't throwing a curve ball, Otis," Pumpsey said. "He's pissed off and he thinks Billy is fucking his sixteen-year-old sister. What are you going to offer him?"

"You let me figure that out. Where do we find this chili pepper?"

"Manny knows where he is. He works in a body shop in

Yuba City."

"So we meet him when he gets off work. He won't want to stir things up with his boss watching. He's not on his home turf. That's important. Believe me, I've been teaching kids like this for the past three years. You want to rattle their cage, you need to do it where it makes them uncomfortable."

"He's not a kid, Otis. He's twenty years old."

"Anybody under twenty-five is a kid, Pumpsey. You're a kid."

"So we do this? You're with us?"

"The brother has a name?"

"Gregorio."

"Tomorrow afternoon we go see him. You guys show up here, I'll talk to Manny. He can find out when the shop closes."

"I knew we could count on you," Pumpsey said.

Otis watched from the landing as they went down the stairs. No you didn't, he thought.

Chapter 44

Pumpsey and Darryl showed up at Otis's place in mid-afternoon and they all drove to Yuba City. Manny had arranged with Otis to meet at the body shop where the brother worked. Five-thirty, Manny said. So the four of them were waiting in the parking lot when Gregorio Lopez came out of the shop. Manny pointed. "That's him," he said.

"You Gregorio Lopez?" Otis asked.

Lopez stopped. "Who wants to know?" he said.

"Gregorio Lopez," Otis repeated. "When I played baseball in West Texas, the name Gregorio Cortez was famous. A real hero. Took a hundred Texas Rangers to corner him."

"What is this," Lopez said, "a fucking history lesson? Who the fuck are you?"

"Somebody who has your best interest at heart."

"I don't know who the fuck you are." He looked at the others. "I don't know who the fuck any of you are," and he went past Otis.

"You have a sister," Otis said.

Lopez stopped, turned, and stared at him. "What's my sister got to do with anything?"

"She's sweet on a friend of ours."

"Who the fuck are you?" This time the voice was angry, strident.

"We're friends of the young man who thinks highly of your sister."

"You know that prick? The whitey baseball player? Tell him he comes within a hundred yards of my sister and I'll break his fucking arm."

"That must be a favorite word of yours," Otis said.

"What word?"

"Fuck. You think that's what the baseball player is doing with your sister?"

"He does that and I'll break more than his fucking arm."

"How are you going to stop that from happening?"

"He wants to throw a baseball again, he'll keep away from her."

"You told him that?"

"I told Rosa to tell him and I told Rosa to keep away from him and you can tell your pussy friend the same thing."

"You think that's going to do it? So maybe you have to break his arm. What's that going to get you? She's going to be pissed off at you, run to take care of him. Exactly what you don't want to happen. How about a sympathy fuck, Lopez? That sound about right to you?"

"How come four of you guys show up? You going to beat me up? Is that the idea?"

"Not if you're as smart as I think you are. We have a mutual interest here, Gregorio. We want the kid to keep pitching. We play ball with him. You want to protect your sister. That's good. She's sixteen. You know Manny, here?" Otis pointed to Manny, who was leaning on the fender of the car. "He's a cop in Oroville."

"Wrong city," Lopez said.

"No, wrong city, right job. All he has to do is make a phone call. How would you like *La Migra* to suddenly come down on Knight's Landing? Immigration cops all over the place. And everybody in town knows you're the one who brought them. To use your favorite word, it would fuck up a lot of families."

"You think I'm supposed to step aside and let this guy put his fucking hands on my sister? You got another think coming, asshole."

"*Señora de compañia.*"

"What the fuck are you talking about?"

"You know what I'm talking about. Somebody who's there when your sister is with Billy."

"Are you out of your fucking mind?"

"No. My guess is that your sister has a good friend. Somebody she hangs out with. And every time your sister and Billy are together, there's her friend. Maybe a boyfriend of hers, too."

Lopez looked at Otis, then at Pumpsey and Darryl. He shifted his gaze to Manny who smiled and nodded his head.

"He touches my sister and he's dead meat," he said, but the vehemence had disappeared from his voice.

"All you have to do is explain things to your sister. We explain them to Billy, and we're all home free," Otis said. "Your sister is sixteen. Billy Collins may be a nineteen-year-old baseball pitcher but he's a fourteen-year-old when it comes to girls. Rosa tells him he has to double date with her friend and he'll jump at the chance. You get to play big brother and you never have to look at us again."

Jesus, Pumpsey thought, he's really fucking big. Otis towered over Lopez who suddenly seemed smaller than he was.

"Looks like we all win this time," Otis said. "It's a fucking home run, Lopez."

On the way back to Oroville, Pumpsey said, "You going to explain this to Billy?"

"No, you get to do that," Otis said.

"You think Billy will agree?"

"Billy isn't stupid. And if he cops a feel while the girlfriend isn't looking, who's to know? The first of November is a long way off, Pumpsey."

Chapter 45

Dutch watched Pumpsey go into his Ricky Henderson crouch. The first pitch came in shoulder high and the umpire called a strike. Pumpsey stepped out of the batter's box, turned and Dutch could clearly hear him.

"A strike? I was looking straight at it. When is that a strike?"

Careful, Dutch thought. Argue with the ump over a call and you can get the gate. He leaned forward, ready to put the brakes on things if they got out of hand.

"Right now, you standing there," the ump said, "that ball is on the letters."

"I don't bat standing up," Pumpsey protested.

"You squat like that with your freaking chest on your knees, I'm not gonna shrink the zone. Play ball," and he crouched down behind the catcher's shoulders.

Pumpsey still stood just outside the box.

"Ricky Henderson never got a call like that," he said,

"This ain't the big leagues, hot dog," the ump said. "In case you didn't notice, your left fielder is a sheetrocker. He did my kitchen last week. Now play ball or take a hike."

Pumpsey pounded the plate twice with his bat and went

into the exaggerated crouch again. This time the pitch was in the dirt.

Dutch leaned back. He looked down the bench to where Otis was talking to Billy. Darryl was unbuckling his shin guards, getting ready to bat, and Dutch heard the umpire call another ball. He wiped his hand twice across his chest, touched his cap. Take the next pitch, he signed, but Pumpsey wasn't looking at him. No point in giving Pumpsey the sign, he thought. He never looks at it anyway.

Otis stood and came down the dugout, and sat next to Dutch.

"The kid says he's working on a new pitch," he said.

"What kind of a pitch?"

"It's a riser. He says he can nail a beer can at ninety feet and it comes up so fucking fast you can't track it."

"You believe that?"

"He's a freak, Dutch. A Hallowe'en spook."

"I heard through the grapevine," Dutch said. "that you and some of the guys went over to Yuba City and did some fancy footwork for the kid. Got his girlfriend's brother to back off."

"Nothing special." Otis said. "We just talked to him."

"The word I got was that you did the talking."

"I'm a teacher, Dutch. That's what I do for a living."

"You didn't need to talk to the brother."

"There's a whole lot of things I do that I don't need to do. You just gave Pumpsey the sign to take the pitch. You didn't need to do that. He's gonna pretend he's Ricky Henderson and he's going to get a walk but you did it anyway. That's what I did in Yuba City."

"Bullshit," Dutch said. "You went up there because a teammate needed your help. You don't fool me."

"I doubt if anybody fools you, Dutch. You're too fucking

old to get fooled."

"This is a team, Otis."

"It's a baseball team, Dutch. What's new about that?"

"Sometimes you got nine guys who go out onto the field at the same time and come in and bat in the same order but they aren't a team. They're just nine guys who wear the same uniform. And sometimes you get nine guys who care about each other, who watch each other's back. You've seen it. Some asshole pitcher deliberately beans somebody and the bench empties. You ever watch that happen, Otis?"

"I've watched it happen. I usually tried to stay out of it. It's easy to get something busted when guys wearing spikes are piling on each other."

"Some clubs never go onto the field like that. They're just nine guys who play ball together. You going up to Yuba City to talk to the punk brother. That's the same thing as going on the field to protect a teammate. I've coached a hundred teams in my life and they rarely become a team. Once in a blue moon something gels and they come together. You guys are a team."

"Pay me my hundred bucks for three innings, Dutch. That's all I ask."

"Bullshit. You got sucked in. Like it or not, Otis, you're part of a team."

"I start the fourth inning?" Otis asked.

"You're a hard case, Otis," Dutch said. "But I got your number." He looked out to where Pumpsey was trotting down to first base.

"Now," he said, "I give him the sign to steal. Which he doesn't need. He'll do it anyway. *Zol es brenning,*" Dutch said. "The hell with it. He's on his own."

Chapter 46

Ray noticed that more than half the fans who now packed the ballpark on Friday and Saturday nights were Hispanic. Much of Knight's Landing was Mexican-American or from the Dominican Republic or Costa Rica. There was a big contingent from Puerto Rico, and Spanish was the language that echoed from the stands. Most of the families worked on the big farms that surrounded Knight's Landing, many working on the tomato picking machines. They were big motorized contraptions, fifty feet long, each one with a driver, a supervisor, and fourteen sorters, usually women. The machines lopped off the tomato plants and scooped them up, and then a conveyor belt brought them between the two rows of women who discarded plants and dirt clods, and left the tomatoes to roll into bins at the end. It was mindless physical work that began at sunup and continued on into the hundred degree afternoons. Huge trucks carried the red cargo to Davis to the Heinz plant or off to distribution centers up and down the Valley. Some of the men worked in the rice fields, drove harvesters, spent hot days opening and closing irrigation ditches. In the fall when the fruit trees were heavy, they operated machines that shook the fruit loose, packed boxes with plums and almonds and peaches and pears. On Friday nights, the work week over, the ballpark took on a festive air. Mariachi music blared from radios in the parking lot, and Ray discovered that Corona beer and limes were a big seller.

It was on the first of September that he decided to have a fan appreciation night. He told Ava he was renting a big tent and Maria Lopez and her husband would set up tables and serve free tacos.

What Ray had noticed was that there was a sizeable group in Knight's Landing who were fans of Lobos de Arecibo, a team in the Puerto Rico winter *beisbol* league. Dennis Huajardo, the third baseman, had played for the Arecibo Wolves, and the fans not only identified with Dennis, but also with the name of the Dog Sox. The black labs on the uniforms and caps were, many of them claimed, actually wolves.

"You're going to give out free food?" Ava said, incredulously.

"Maybe five hundred tacos, fireworks at the seventh inning stretch," Ray said. "Beers at two for the price of one, but they'll drink more Coronas than you can count. We'll break even and you'll be the queen of the night. *La Reina de la noche.*"

"And we'll have a ballpark full of drunks. Jesus, Ray, are you out of your mind?"

"That's entirely possible," Ray said. "But it will be a party the town won't forget, and the snack shack already burned down, so there's not much else they can ruin."

People started arriving an hour before game time and by the end of the first inning Frank Gates, the liquor store owner, had gone back to his store for a dozen more cases of beer. When Ray announced the opening lineups, a cheer went up for three players on the Yuba City team. They all had Hispanic names and Ray looked up into the stands where a sizeable group of men, already well oiled, were waving a huge Mexican flag.

The stands along the third base line were packed with Arecibo fans who cheered everything Dennis Huajardo did. By the top of the fourth inning, a chant of *Ahr rey-see-bo! Ahe rey see bo*! could be heard on the highway and across the river. The Puerto Rico flag waved above the shouting crowd and then two boys came out of the stands, holding the flag staff, waving it back and forth, trotting down the third base line toward the left field corner. The flag was red-and-white striped with a single white star in the center of a blue triangle. The Mexican Flag began to wave frantically. three panels of green and white and red, and the chant, *Meh hee co! Meh hee co!* drowned out the Puerto Ricans. Ava turned to Ray. She bent close and shouted in his ear, "Five more innings to go, *El Jéfe*, Have you got a plan?"

He looked at her, shook his head, no. Behind them the Puerto Ricans were outshouting the Mexicans and things were beginning to fly. On the field the Yuba City batter hit a sharp grounder to third. Dennis fielded it, stepped on the bag, forcing the runner on second and then whipped the ball to first. Johnny Hardcase stretched, and the runner was out by half a step, ending the inning. The boys with the Puerto Rico flag ran onto the field, trailed by a dozen kids and a few drunk men, rounding the bases. At third base they met the Mexican flag and things began to get ugly. Half-empty beer cups, tacos, and a few bottles rained down on the field.

Ray got up and headed for the closet behind the stands where the public address microphone was. On the way he saw the kid in the dog suit, holding the head under his arm, looking scared.

"Take down the flag!" Ray yelled at him, pointing to the American flag that hung limply from the flag pole behind home plate. He detoured to the tent where Maria and José were making tacos. A line of people stood waiting.

"No more beer," Ray said. He took José by the arm and led him out of the tent. "The fireworks," Ray said. "I want them to go off now!"

"It is not the seventh inning," Jose said.

"I know," Ray said, "but I want them to go off now. And like last time, all at once. Can you find your brother and get it done?"

Behind them the crowd was louder, and more men had joined the melee at third base. José nodded and ran off in the direction of the rice silos.

The kid in the dog suit came up to Ray with the flag draped over his paws.

"Get somebody to help you," Ray said. "One of the ballplayers. Get Manny Garcia. Go out into center field and wave the flag, And when the music starts, hold it up high."

He went to the closet, opened it, and turned on the P.A. system. He put in a CD, and punched the play button. The loudspeakers crackled and the Spanish version of *The Star Spangled Banner* boomed out.

Amanece: lo véis a la luz de la aurora.

In center field the boy in the dog suit had his head on again and Manny Garcia had the other end of the flag, holding it high above their heads. Suddenly the sky was lit with rockets and the combination of explosions and the crackling Spanish words drowned out the noise from the crowd. And then, slowly, the voices in the stands joined in. The Puerto Rican and Mexican flags continued to wave, but the third base combatants came to attention. The fireworks and the song faded at about the same time, and there was silence in the park. The last sparks from the rockets trailed down, winking out in the blackness beyond the river.

Then the plate ump yelled "Play ball!" and the crowd

erupted in another cheer.

When Ray found his chair next to Ava, she leaned over and said, "Nice work, El Jéfe. Now what happens?"

"I turned off the beer faucet," Ray said. "Now we cross our fingers."

The cheers went back and forth between the Yuba City Mexican contingent and the Knights Landing Arecibo fans until Billy took the mound at the top of the seventh. The Dog Sox had a one run lead and when Billy went into his first windup, the crowd let out a hoarse shout. The ball came up across the letters and the ump raised his right hand, punching the air. Ray looked again at the stands and he realized that although Billy wasn't Mexican and he wasn't Puerto Rican, he was a freak, and those people, who were always on the fringe, felt an affinity with this string-bean oddity who threw a *beisbol* in a way that no one else did.

He leaned over and spoke into Ava's ear. "We're home free," he said. "It's Billy-magic time."

It tuned out that Rosa and José had given away six hundred tacos but the beer sales had been more than Ray expected, even though he had cut it off at the fourth inning. Subtract the beer sales from the tent and the fireworks and the tacos and he came out eight hundred dollars in the red, but he wasn't about to tell Ava how much they had lost. He would make it up out of his own pocket.

"It was a good night," he said to Ava as they walked to the car. Jack had spent the game hiding under a table in the tent near Maria.

"So what kind of a score do I get for this night of mayhem?" he asked.

"On a scale of zero to one hundred, this rates as a ninety nine for idiocy," she said. "But you get points for the fireworks and the Spanish anthem. Exactly what is the translation of those words?"

"It's sort of, Wake up do you see by the light of the moon?"

"Sounds like something I might have said to you."

"You want to try that again?"

"With or without the fireworks?"

"I might have a rocket left," Ray said.

"As long as you don't sing while it's going off," Ava replied.

* * * * * *

Ray got up and opened the door of the bathroom. Jack came out and lay at the foot of the bed. When Ray got back in, he said, "About tonight. It wasn't the brightest thing I've done. We lost some money, but I'll make it up. I thought it was a good idea."

"You had no idea you'd start a baseball war."

"The two-for-one beer thing was a no-brainer."

Ava smoothed his hair back from his forehead. She took one of his hands and placed it on her chest. "Heartbeat," she said. "Can you feel it?"

"Yes."

"I'm alive. You're alive." She nodded toward the end of the bed. "Jack is still alive. Nobody died tonight."

"Sometimes," Ray said, "I look in the mirror and I say to myself, what does she see in me? I'm an ordinary looking guy, and I'm not rich or famous and you're this fucking beautiful woman who could have anybody you want, but here we are. Sometimes I think I'll wake up and you won't be here."

"I get hit on by good-looking men all the time, Ray. Sharp-looking lawyers who think they're God's gift to women. They think a hundred dollar haircut and a thousand dollar Armani suit will catch my eye. That I'm just dying to climb into their Mercedes. But none of them ever made me cabinets with their own hands, or bought me a baseball team, or took me to Tiffany's to try on expensive jewelry. And if I had said to you, 'I want this one,' you would have mortgaged your life to buy it for me. That much I know. You're a nice-looking guy. Ray Adams. But your good looks are mostly on the inside, where it counts. I'm not going to disappear on you. You're not going to wake up in the morning and find me gone."

"I was afraid you would disappear in the river the other night."

"But you were waiting there to pull me out. If I had called for help, you would have jumped in, even thought you probably would have drowned. And I'll forgive you for losing my beer."

She reached up and smoothed his hair back from his forehead.

"You're a handsome man, Ray Adams, Don't you ever forget that."

Chapter 47

Darryl had dozed off in front of the TV when he vaguely heard the dim sound. It was a soft thump followed by another one, and occasionally a grunted "Yes!" The sounds came from the back yard.

The blinds on the sliding glass door were broken and Darryl had to raise the edge to look out. There, in the light of the single backyard floodlight, Billy was standing next to a bucket of old baseballs. Far down at the corner of the yard was what looked like the figure of a man, standing still, not moving. Billy wound up and the familiar motion swept the grass at his feet. The thump came again, but the figure had not moved.

Darryl slid the door open.

"Billy?" he said.

Billy turned. "What's up?" he said.

"That's what I was going to ask." As Darryl stepped out onto the small landing, he could see that the figure of a man was an outline, life-sized, pinned to an old mattress that leaned against the corner of the fence.

"What the hell is that?" Darryl asked.

"It's a target. Manny got it for me. They use them at the

police academy for target practice. I got a bunch of them."

"And what, exactly, are you doing?"

"Practicing my new pitch. It's a riser. Watch this." Billy turned, put his foot back against a mound of dirt that had been scraped up and went into the windup. Darryl watched but in the half-dark he couldn't see the ball, only the impact as it hit the figure just above the belt. It was, he realized, a pitch that was faster than anything Billy had thrown at him so far.

"How fast you think that is?" he asked.

"Maybe the nineties," Billy said.

Maybe more than that, Darryl thought

"It's like a split-finger fastball, but I release it sideways," Billy said. "You know how the split-finger dives off to one side?"

Darryl nodded.

"Well this one dives up."

He reached into the bucket for another baseball.

"How long you been doing this?" Darryl asked.

"About a week. "

"No, I mean how long you been throwing tonight?"

"I don't know. A while."

"Pack it in, Billy."

"Let me finish this bucket."

"No. Give your arm a rest. Come on in. Have a beer."

"One more," Billy said. He reached down and took a ball from the bucket. He wound up and threw. The ball hit the target in the chest so hard that it penetrated the old mattress. Darryl reached inside the door and turned off the outside light and the yard was suddenly plunged into darkness.

"Get your skinny ass in here," he said. "Save that pitch for a game."

Chapter 48

Ava had rented the tiny cottage at Dillon Beach from a woman she knew. It was old and clung to the hillside above the ocean and it was painted an ugly yellow, but it was only a short walk to the beach and at night the sound of the surf was constant, a soothing rhythm.

The first morning Ray woke early. He looked at his watch. It was only five, and when he looked out toward the water it was black, no moon, only a few stars. Ava lay asleep, one arm thrust out, her spiky hair in a tangle, and Ray quietly dressed. He picked up the flashlight and Jack came out of the bathroom, his claws clicking on the linoleum floor. Ray let himself and the dog out, closing the door quietly. He hiked up the street until it ended, then continued on the fire road toward the top of the ridge. There was a fine mist in the air, and it was cold, and he zipped his jacket up, feeling his temples beginning to pound as he climbed. Jack ranged ahead, invisible in the darkness. It took half an hour to reach the top of the ridge where Ray looked out over the water. It was a flat, gun metal grey in the almost-light of dawn. Below were the few lights of the village. One of them was the porch light on the cottage, but he couldn't tell which one it was.

And then, on an impulse, he sat down on a rock outcropping and began to take off his shoes. He unlaced them, placed them side-by-side, took off his socks and tucked them into his shoes. He stood, slipped his pants off and then his shorts. He unzipped the jacket, laid it on the rock and then his shirt and stood, naked, in the cold wind. Jack nosed his legs and then sat, as if expecting Ray to do something more.

What the fuck am I doing? Ray thought. He stretched his arms above his head, and he felt the mist stinging at his chest and his legs and his belly.

This is the kind of thing Ava would do, he thought. Something that has, at this moment, no explanation. Below, a few more lights had winked on. They have no idea, he thought. A naked man is standing up here, facing the sea with a dog sitting next to him, and he imagined Ava standing there, too, only she would be comfortable in what she was doing, and he thought, I have learned something from her. I'm not sure what it is, but this is some secret thing that she has given me.

Suddenly he was very cold, and he bent, picked up his jacket and pulled it on. He dressed quickly. The wind had settled and the mist had turned to a fine rain as he started down the road. I will not tell her what I did, he thought. But it has something to do with her. Some connection. Something has happened to me and I don't want to lose it. It was as if, when he had stripped off his clothes and stood in the biting wind, he had exposed himself to some truth that he could not understand but knew that it was now part of him and he broke into a trot, anxious to return to the cottage where she slept.

There was a light in the cottage when he opened the door. Ava was reading the *New Yorker* in bed, and she looked up.

"Where have you two been?" she asked.

"We took a walk."

"In the dark?"

"It's getting light out. You were asleep. I didn't want to wake you."

"There was an empty space next to me in the bed," she said. "I could feel it. It woke me up."

"I can fix you an omelet," he said.

"You okay?" she asked.

"I'm fine," he said. "Never been better. Top of the ninth and we've got a ten-run lead."

She laid the *New Yorker* on the bedside table. "It looks like the Dog Sox have a new closer," she said. "His name is Ray Adams and the word is he's got a fastball that can't be hit."

She sat up and the blankets dropped into her lap.

"You ready to pitch?" she asked. "You could put the game on ice."

Chapter 49

Dutch checked the field, made sure the foul lines were straight. Sometimes Lenny, who chalked the lines, was a bit unsteady, and there was a waver that was decidedly not regulation. It was hot, and Dutch sat in the dugout and waited for the boys to show.

He looked out at the field, fading green to brown in the September heat, not like the big league fields that were always a rich green. Fielding a ground ball on a surface like this, he thought, was a challenge. Any kid who could handle a hot ball off the infield would find a ballpark in the Bigs a piece of cake. He remembered the afternoon he had trotted out onto the field in Oakland. Twenty-nine years old, and the tail end of the season. He had been called up from Stockton, and he remembered waiting while the announcer called out the lineup. He was in the major leagues and his name had echoed back from the stands and he had gone up the steps onto the grass and trotted out to left field and it was as if the whole world were watching. But it was a Thursday afternoon game and the bleachers were only half-full and when the second batter connected and a long fly ball came toward him. He had drifted back, momentarily losing the ball in the afternoon sun, and then, at the last second, spotting it. It had been an easy out, but he remembered it as the most difficult fly ball he had ever fielded. And when he came to bat, he had fouled off three pitches. He remembered that, too. A fastball, a change-up and another fastball. The curve came, and he was caught off guard and he felt foolish. And he knew that the pitcher had his number.

Some crows had gathered at second base and were picking at the infield. Pumpsey came into the dugout, dropped his bat bag and opened it. He began to rub the handle of one of the bats with rosin and Dutch remembered, oh so many years ago, in some other life, when he had done the same.

"Where's the other two?" he asked.

"They're coming," Pumpsey said, not looking up.

"Billy okay?" Dutch asked.

"Far as I know," Pumpsey said.

"You get two more stolen bases tonight and you have the league record," Dutch said.

"I know that."

"You don't need to look for the sign. You get on base, you go for it." Unnecessary advice, Dutch thought. He's going to go for it whether I give him the sign or not.

There was the sound of the Burrito&Taco wagon driving into the park, and then the first fans started coming through the gate. Otis had materialized at the end of the bench, a book in his lap. Darryl was strapping on his shin guards and Barney went down the first base line with Paul to warm up.

It was a familiar count-down. This has happened a thousand times in my life, Dutch thought. The Marysville Mudhens were on the field taking batting practice, and he heard the crack! of bats and the sound of chatter. I am an old man, Dutch thought. I have waited through ten thousand innings, and now there will be nine more.

Ava appeared behind home plate, a beer in one hand. And the loudspeakers crackled. Ray's voice echoed over the park announcing the lineup, and Dutch thought, this is who I am. He looked down the bench to where Otis had stopped reading and was looking out toward the field.

I'm not like him, Dutch thought. He's not connected to this thing the way I am. He remembered a phrase his father had spoken. *Dos gefelt mir.* This pleases me.

"This pleases me," Dutch said, and Manny, who sat next to him, said, "What did you say, Dutch?"

"Nothing," Dutch said. "I was just talking to myself."

Chapter 50

Ray saw him stumbling along the fence and he thought, the son-of-a-bitch is trying to sneak in. It was Bucky Collins and he sagged against the fence several times, then skidded down into a sitting position. His head lolled onto his chest. Ray thought, let a deputy sheriff cart him off. He found the kid with the dog suit behind the burrito wagon, drinking a beer. The dog head was in his lap and he was leaning against the rear wheel. When he saw Ray, he covered the beer with the dog head and tried to get to his feet.

"Relax," Ray said. "I want you to do something for me." The kid clutched the dog head with both hands.

"I want you to watch somebody for me," Ray said. He reached out his hand and held it until the kid pulled out the half-empty can of beer. Ray set it next to the wheel.

"You can come back for it," Ray said. The kid followed him around the wagon and looked at the slumped figure that Ray pointed at on the far side of the fence.

"Watch him," Ray said, "If he moves, see where he goes."

Ray turned and hurried out the gate into the parking lot. He had left his phone in the glove compartment of his truck and as he threaded his way between pickups and beat-up sedans, he hoped that Bucky Collins would remain against the chain-link fence. "Sorry-ass son-of-a-bitch," he muttered. But he knew that if Bucky Collins revived and somehow showed up on the field, it would be disaster for Billy. He got to his truck, popped the lock, and reached into the glove compartment. He took out his cell phone, punched in the numbers for the sheriff and when the dispatcher answered, he told her what he wanted. A drunk had to be removed from the Knight's Landing baseball park. But she told him that unless his drunk was violent or showing somebody a weapon, no deputy could respond. An accident on Highway 162 had the nearest car tied up.

Ray hung up and went back to where Bobby, holding the dog head under his arm, was watching the back of Bucky Collins' comatose body. Poor fucker, Ray thought.

"He hasn't moved," Bobby said.

"Go finish your beer," Ray said. Bobby looked at him, and Ray added, "Take off the dog suit. You're done for tonight. And that's your last beer here, kid. After this you drink Cokes."

Bobby hurried off and Ray focused on Bucky. He had fallen sideways, and was now nearly lying on the ground. Out like a light, Ray thought. What would it be like to have a father like that. He remembered his own father. He had been a cabinetmaker, and Ray remembered the lessons that his father gave every time they worked on something together. His father measured things in sixty-fourths of an inch. Which side of the line are you going to saw on? he would ask. Remember, the kerf has a thickness. They might have been repairing the fence on the back of the lot behind the little house in the Sunset District, but it made no difference. He remembered his old man at the workbench in the back of the garage on a Saturday morning, sharpening his saws. There were three of them: a rip saw, a cross-cut saw, and a back saw. The rip saw had eight teeth to the inch, the cross-cut had twelve, and the back saw had twenty-one. How many ten-year-olds had known that, he wondered. His father clamped the saw in a vice and then used a tiny triangular file to sharpen the teeth. "If your tools aren't sharp, then you're worthless," his father said. And Ray had learned his craft working with his father until, when he was twenty-one and his father was fifty-one, his old man had suddenly seized up on a job. His heart stopped and Ray was on his own.

He remembered lunches on the job, sitting with a sandwich and a pickle and the smell of sawdust or wood shavings. His father had made the lunches, and the sandwiches were as neat as the cabinets he made, meticulously put together, the tomatoes sliced exactly the same thickness. Nothing fell out of a sandwich his father had made.

Ray looked again at Bucky Collins. He was lying on his side, his face buried in the grass. What would it have been like to have a father who only taught you how to punch a woman or a kid? Somebody who was good at disappearing from your life. Better not to have one at all. He walked to the fence, pushed with the toe of his shoe at the back of the body lying against it. The body didn't move. Bucky Collins wasn't going any place, that seemed sure. Ray turned and went to find the empty chair next to Ava.

Chapter 51

Bucky Collins crawled out of his hole at the top of the seventh inning. There he was, dirty and drunk, grass and leaves stuck to the side of his face, leaning against the left-field end of the visitors' dugout, wearing a shit-eating grin. Billy saw him and stood, hands at his sides, staring. At first Dutch didn't see him and wondered what Billy was doing, but when he followed Billy's gaze, he saw Bucky take off his baseball cap and tip it toward the mound. He put the cap back on, started toward the baseline, stumbled, and then stopped. By now the crowd was focused on him.

Shit, Dutch thought. Isaac and Aaron didn't get it done.

Then he saw Billy put his right foot against the rubber, still facing third base. He bent forward, as if he were looking at Darryl for the sign. He straightened, his arm came up and started around and Dutch held his breath. It was the windup to end all windups, and when Billy released the ball, his body was almost flat out, coming off the mound, his right arm fully extended.

The pitch was a low fastball that skimmed the ground and then, at the last second, rose to strike Bucky Collins in the chest with so much force that it knocked him backwards. The crowd let out a collective gasp. Billy raised his arm and pointed at the unconscious Bucky, stabbing his finger at him. Dutch remembered that Dennis Eckersley had done that whenever he struck out a batter for the A's. Two ballplayers came out of the visitors' dugout to look at Bucky and they turned and yelled something. Dutch was frozen, leaning over the dugout railing, and then there was a commotion as somebody came out of the stands. It was Doc Pickens, the old general practitioner who had been the only doctor in Knight's Landing for as long as anybody could remember. He bent over the unconscious Bucky, turning his head upward to say something to the circle of people who had gathered. The ballpark waited. Billy looked toward home plate and held up his mitt. He wanted another ball. Darryl looked at him, turned to the home plate umpire and held out his hand. The ump paused, looked down toward third base, then toward the mound. Billy still held his mitt out. The ump put a ball in Darryl's hand and he tossed it softly out to the mound. He crouched and made the sign for a fastball. The batter stayed out of the box, still looking toward third base. Billy wound up and the ball came in, a perfect pitch, rising, powering into Darryl's mitt.

By now the crowd could hear the siren of the volunteer fire department truck. A sheriff's cruiser had pulled into the parking lot. Bucky Collins was conscious, had vomited several times, and was propped against the end of the visitors' dugout.

Ray was suddenly at Dutch's side.

"What the fuck was that all about?" he asked.

"I believe," Dutch said, "that our Bucky troubles are over. And if the plate ump has any sense of justice at all, he'll call that a strike."

Chapter 52

The season ended with a string of four wins and the Dog Sox took the Central Valley League pennant. A scout from the Oakland A's came to watch Billy pitch the last two games and then he and Dutch went out for a beer.

"I played with the A's for a week," Dutch said. "It was their first year in Oakland. They brought me up from Stockton the last week of the season. I found out I couldn't hit a big-league curve ball."

"Who do I talk to about your submarine whiz kid?"

"Me. I found him. I say what happens to him. The owner gives me the nod."

"As a closer, he looks like the real thing."

"He is," Dutch said. "Solid gold."

"Front office likes him. You guys got him under contract?"

"Only for this season, but we've got an option for next year. You'd have to buy that out."

"Who decides that?"

"I do. And there's one thing more."

"Which is?"

"You take the kid, you take me, too."

The scout raised his beer, looked at Dutch in the mirror at the back of the bar. What he saw was an old man with rounded shoulders, white hair, and a leathery face from too many summers in the sun.

"I want one season on the bench in the Bigs," Dutch said. "It won't cost you much. You take the kid, I come along. I won't butt into anybody's business. I'll keep an eye on the kid and at the end of the season you can wave goodbye to me. Take it or leave it."

"Or I go talk to your owner and offer her enough money for that option to make her mouth water."

"You could try that. It would be cheaper to put me on the end of the bench in your dugout."

That winter, Ava sold the Dog Sox to Frank Gates, the liquor store owner in Knight's Landing. The A's paid her five thousand dollars for Billy's option, Gates paid three thousand for the team rights and all the equipment, and she got fifteen hundred from the insurance company for the burned-out Snack Shack. On her birthday she called Ray and told him to meet her at the entrance to the Stockton Garage in San Francisco. They walked to Tiffany's and after trying on one necklace after another, Ava bought an emerald pendant on a gold chain for nine thousand, four hundred dollars.

When they came out onto Post Street in the cold January sun, the emerald pendant on the gold chain glittered against her white chest. She took the remaining hundred dollar bill from her purse and stuffed it into Ray's shirt pocket.

"Now we go drink some champagne," she said, "and then you get to fuck my lights out."

Epilogue

The Oakland A's gave Dutch Goltz a contract as a pitching coach for a season. He got thirty-five thousand to sit on the far end of the bench and keep an eye on Billy Collins. But as the season wore on, young players began to drift toward him. They called him Gramps and they sat next to the seventy-three year old man because they learned that he would tell a story and they would learn how to spot a pickoff or maybe shift a foot to get a better look at the pitch. One kid who had gone zero for fifteen listened while Dutch told him about being a rookie who couldn't hit a major-league curve ball and how, if the kid closed his back eye at batting practice, it would force him to follow the ball all the way in. The kid got a hit the next night.

Billy Collins, the poet, came to Oakland to watch his namesake pitch, and he wrote a poem about the game. It began:

Last night I pitched three innings
for the Oakland A's
I was brilliant.

It was better than being poet laureate
of the whole world.

Dutch kept an eye on Billy, and enrolled him in a yoga class.

Billy Collins pitched 63 innings that year, had 21 saves and an ERA of 0.62, which was the same number as the age of the stylishly grey-haired woman Dutch met at the synagogue.

The A's went to the World Series where Billy Collins closed out three games without giving up a run. Billy and Dutch both went home with a World Series ring. Aaron and Isaac still met on Friday mornings at the synagogue to make bread. "*A mentsh tracht und Gott lacht,*" Isaac said. *A person plans and God laughs.* Aaron nodded.

Otis Bickford sold his novel about a small-town baseball team to Random House. Twentieth Century Fox picked up the film rights.

Ray married Ava and they rented an old stone house in Italy for their honeymoon where they drank champagne in the warm evenings and then walked through the meadow below the house. Ray wore a pair of old khaki trousers and Ava wore a white shirt of Ray's. They wore nothing else.

"One complete outfit between the two of us ought to be enough," Ava said.

Jack, the dog, lay on the warm terrace of the old stone house and waited for them to return.

Bucky Collins got run over by a ranch truck while crossing the highway in Knight's Landing.

Caravel Books is a crime and mystery imprint of Pleasure Boat Studio: A Literary Press. Our other Caravel books are as follows:

Music of the Spheres * Michael Burke * $16

Swan Dive * Michael Burke * $15

The Lord God Bird * Russell Hill * $15 * Nominated for an
    Edgar Award

Island of the Naked Women * Inger Frimansson, trans. by Laura
    Wideburg * $18

The Shadow in the Water * Inger Frimansson, trans. by Laura
    Wideburg * $18 * Winner of Best Swedish Mystery 2005

Good Night, My Darling * Inger Frimansson, trans. by Laura
    Wideburg * $16 * Winner of Best Swedish Mystery 1998
    Winner of Best Translation Prize from ForeWord Magazine
    2007

The Case of Emily V. * Keith Oatley * $18 * Commonwealth
    Writers Prize for Best First Novel

Homicide My Own * Anne Argula * $16 * Nominated for an
    Edgar Award

Orders: Pleasure Boat Studio books are available by order from your bookstore, directly from our website, or through the following:
SPD (Small Press Distribution), Partners/West, Baker & Taylor, Ingram, and Amazon.com or Barnesandnoble.com

  and directly from us at
Pleasure Boat Studio: A Literary Press
201 West 89th Street
New York, NY 10024
Tel / Fax: 8888105308
www.pleasureboatstudio.com / pleasboat@nyc.rr.com